How to Handle
an Ancestry Scandal

A MAGS AND BIDDY GENEALOGY MYSTERY
BOOK THREE

ELIZA WATSON

How to Handle an Ancestry Scandal

Copyright © 2021 by Elizabeth Watson

All rights reserved by author.

Cover design by Lyndsey Lewellen at LLewellen Designs

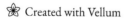 Created with Vellum

Books by Eliza Watson

NONFICTION

Genealogy Tips & Quips

FICTION

A Mags and Biddy Genealogy Mystery Series

How to Fake an Irish Wake (Book 1)

How to Snare a Dodgy Heir (Book 2)

How to Handle an Ancestry Scandal (Book 3)

How to Spot a Murder Plot (Book 4)

How to Trace a Cold Case (Book 5)

The Travel Mishaps of Caity Shaw Series

Flying by the Seat of My Knickers (Book 1)

Up the Seine Without a Paddle (Book 2)

My Christmas Goose Is Almost Cooked (Book 3)

My Wanderlust Bites the Dust (Book 4)

Live to Fly Another Day (Book 5)

When in Doubt Don't Chicken Out (Book 6)

FOR ADDITIONAL BOOKS VISIT

WWW.ELIZAWATSON.COM.

Dear Reader,

My obsession with cemeteries began when I spent a college semester at the Sorbonne in Paris. I enjoyed many quiet afternoons studying at the Montmartre cemetery with my furry friends—the dozens of cats residing there. That was when I first encountered Louise Thouret, who died in 1856 at the age of sixteen. Her grave boasted an elaborate white marble sculpture of a girl resting her head on a pillow, a sheet tucked up to her nightgown's neckline. A bouquet of flowers sat on her grave.

Who had placed fresh flowers on Louise's grave when she'd died over a century ago? What had caused her death at such a young age? Was she from a prestigious family, having such an elaborate grave? I had no clue how to obtain answers to all the questions racing through my mind. In the early 1990s, the internet was still in its infancy, and Ancestry.com wouldn't yet launch for a few years. In 2007 I embarked on my genealogy journey after visiting my ancestors' homeland, Ireland. However, Louise Thouret and Paris's cemeteries had sparked my interest in ancestry research fifteen years earlier without me even realizing it.

Cemeteries are an integral part of the plot in *How to Handle an Ancestry Scandal*. At the end of the story, I've included two articles from my nonfiction book *Genealogy Tips & Quips*: "Walking Among the Dead—What a Cemetery Can Tell You About Your Ancestors' Lives" and "Become a Cemetery Whisperer." I hope you find the research tips helpful.

Have fun in Ireland with Mags and Biddy. As always, there is sure to be plenty of shenanigans!

Eliza Watson

To Bernard and Nuala Bolger

*Thanks so much for being such an important part
of my Coffey ancestry journey!*

Acknowledgments

Our Ireland home is an 1887 renovated schoolhouse in my Coffey ancestors' hometown in County Westmeath, the setting for Mags's new home. The place is surviving the pandemic thanks to our wonderful neighbor friends Des, Mags, and Darragh Carter. Ireland is a beautiful country with hundreds of sites to visit, but the best part is spending time with family and friends.

A special thank you to Dr. Mohd Fazly Helmi at the Regional Hospital Mullingar, Ireland, for answering my numerous questions about crime scene and medical procedures. Any errors in this story are on me, not him. Thanks to Nikki Ford for your in-depth feedback as usual. Also to beta readers Judy Watson and Sandra Watson for all the wonderful input. To Dori Harrell for your fab editorial skills. To Ray Dittmeier for your final proofreading tweaks. Thanks to you two, I can publish a book with confidence. To Lyndsey Lewellen for another brilliant cover and capturing the spirit of Mags and Biddy.

One

A SCREAM SHRILLED from inside my house and out the open conservatory door.

The elderly reunion attendees in my backyard stopped chatting, and their gazes darted to the former Ballycaffey National Schoolhouse—which I'd inherited six months ago from my late grandmother. My best friend, Biddy McCarthy, and I hiked up our sundresses and took off running toward my yellow cottage. Flip-flops slapped against the soles of our feet. Biddy's long blond ponytail swung in the air. A clump of my brown hair came loose from its clip. We raced past picnic tables while assuring guests everything was fine. Yet I feared that three quiet months without any mysteries to solve was about to come to an end.

Biddy and I flew through the conservatory and skidded to a stop at the kitchen doorway. Rosie Connelly, an elderly woman in a lavender dress and a pearl necklace, was shaking a wooden spoon and shouting profanities. Her anger was directed at Pinky—a large sheep with a splash of pink dye on his cream-colored wool. The animal had apparently knocked three pie tins off the white countertop and was scarfing up globs of strawberry-rhubarb pie filling from the wood floor.

"Janey," Biddy muttered.

A crowd joined us, staring in shock at prim and proper Rosie cussing up a storm. The rogue sheep continued enjoying the pie. The animal spent more time in my yard than his owner's field, but this was the first time he'd been so bold as to enter my house. Edmond Collier, Rosie's boyfriend, gently slipped the spoon from the woman's grip and tried to calm her down. Rosie's cooking and baking had put some needed weight on the tall man.

"Well, that's downright disappointing." Gretta Lynch shook her head. "Was hoping for some excitement." The thin woman in a light-gray dress turned and stalked out, her silver-haired bun secured tightly.

Not a paid detective, I didn't go looking for crimes to solve. If they came to me, that was a different story.

Last month, while Gretta was on road-rubbish duty—community service work for her role in Finn O'Brien's car accident—she'd reported a suspicious windowless white van cruising the roads of Ballycaffey. Her tip had led to the guards busting a theft ring that had sheds full of stolen lawn mowers and outdoor equipment. Thankfully, my new red riding lawn mower hadn't been a victim.

I grabbed a box of Froot Loops from the cupboard and shook it. The sheep swiveled its head in my direction and eyed the box. I left a trail of colorful cereal pieces from the kitchen floor through the conservatory and to the back-yard. Pinky followed, inhaling his favorite treat and stopping to drink rainwater from a pan on the conservatory's tile floor. Rain was always in Ireland's forecast, so the pan was a permanent fixture until the leaking roof was replaced.

Once outside, I scolded the sheep. A sense of pride rose inside me for taking a stand with the animal. Not long ago, if I'd found him in my kitchen, I'd have raced from the house and kept on running up the road to the safety of McCarthy's pub—owned by Biddy's parents.

I sent the curious guests to the backyard and then headed inside, closing the conservatory door behind me. I threw my hair back up in the clip and heaved a sigh. In my small lemon-colored kitchen, Rosie was in tears, kneeling on the floor, scooping up globs of pie filling with her hands and whipping it into empty pie tins. I joined Edmond in assisting her with the cleanup and providing words of comfort.

"There are still plenty of pies to go around," Biddy assured Rosie while slicing one. Twenty-two strawberry-rhubarb, cherry, and elderberry pies lined the countertop. "We'll just have to slice them in eight pieces instead of six."

I should have been in tears like Rosie, since I'd been part of the two-day pie-baking marathon. However, I was just relieved not to have found a dead body lying on my kitchen floor. Had I been a few seconds later, there might have been a dead *sheep* in my kitchen. Rosie would have been the last person I'd have ever suspected of murder. Until ten minutes ago, I'd also never thought her capable of winning a cussing match with several regulars at McCarthy's pub. It just went to show you never knew what someone was capable of until put in the position.

Rosie had come to my baking rescue after I'd been unable to master Grandma's flaky crust. If I wanted to one day pass along the secret recipe and pie-baking tradition to my children, I needed to know how to *bake* them. I trusted Rosie not to divulge the coveted recipe.

Tommy Lynch, a gray-haired man with a bit of a belly and happy brown eyes, wandered into the kitchen holding a beer. "Not worth replacing the windows with moisture between the glass until ye build a new conservatory. I could be putting a bid in on the project, if ye'd like."

Right now?

Pie filling oozed between my fingers and plopped onto the wood floor.

"My man down in Castleroche would give ye a fine deal on the windows. And Jimmy Cavanaugh is brilliant. Built our new conservatory a few years back. And ye could use the room in cooler weather, if I'd be installing radiators."

For once I didn't have any urgent home repairs. I had the money to replace Grandma's mail-order conservatory with a permanent structure. Three months ago, my genealogy business had taken off after my appearance on the *Rags to Riches Roadshow*. Biddy and I'd gone on the antique show to discuss our role in locating a missing person, Aidan Neil, and his family heirloom—an unpublished manuscript involving prominent Irish author Brendan Quigley. Thanks to the show, dozens of clients had hired me to locate wills and probate records to help them prove provenance of heirlooms or uncover the rightful owners. My discoveries had started at least two family feuds.

"That'd be great if you could provide an estimate."

Tommy smiled. "And should ye ever be needing a stove, call in to me shop. Will be giving ye a fine deal." He strolled out through the conservatory, analyzing the structure.

The green cast-iron stove tucked into the yellow living

room's brick fireplace had been a trooper this past winter. It had puffed out peat and warmed the place when my radiators had been on the fritz and the fuel tank was damaged. Should it need replacing, it'd be my cheapest home repair yet.

Biddy and I each carried a tray with four sliced pies outside to the dessert table. Two elderly women were discussing the recent theft ring while Gretta smiled proudly.

This was Gretta's first reunion. Unlike her husband, Tommy, she hadn't gone to school in Ballycaffey. She'd never been friendly with the locals, including Biddy and me, until recently assisting us with the Neil mystery. After eighteen years, she appeared to have somewhat forgiven us for clear-cutting her daffodils when we were eight. She was a new woman, and the entire town had Biddy and me to thank.

"Still surprised that it didn't turn out to be Peggy Ryan who nicked the lawn equipment," Biddy said. "Now that she's head of Castleroche's TidyTown committee, she'd be wanting Ballycaffey out of the running. The woman is fiercely competitive."

"I had a sensor light installed on the shed," one woman said. "Every passing tractor and Guinness truck set it off until it was properly adjusted."

I inhaled the calming scent of freshly mowed grass, happy my mower was safely tucked away in the shed. It was paid off, as was my home's new fuel tank. Two years ago, all the fuel on my road had been stolen. The thief had drilled a hole near the bottom of the tank, which my grandma had plugged up. I really needed to look at having a shed constructed to protect the tank.

Gretta and the ladies walked off with pieces of pie.

Biddy peered across the yard at Evelyn McCreery, the

school's former teacher, taking Aileen and Mickey Molloy's annual photo under the ash tree where the couple had shared their first kiss at the age of ten. The tree was home to my fairy house, where two wishes impatiently waited for the fairies to grant them.

"Aileen is now selling her knitted goat apparel," Biddy said. "Bet she could be making a sweater for Pinky."

The naughty sheep was now sleeping under the wooden trellis with a rosebush climbing up the latticework. He'd stopped stripping the bush of its leaves and had eaten the tops off the pansies I'd planted in front of the wooden patio.

"Hope she's knitting slippers for her goat who about broke my back." My shoulder was still out of whack from Aileen's baby goat using my back as a springboard six months ago.

"Speaking of Mickey, are ya ready for your date with Finn this weekend?"

Finn O'Brien was the son of Mickey's first cousin, a pub owner in Drumcara, a nearby village. I'd met both men after Finn showed up at my door at Christmastime searching for his biological father, whom he'd found thanks to my assistance and in part to Mickey and Evelyn. Finn had declined my invite to the reunion. His family-owned woolen goods business in Wexford was in the process of opening their sixth shop, located in County Clare. Like me, work was eating up his spare time.

"It's not a date." Even though I'd bought a new sundress and sandals for the dinner and smiled at the mention of his name. My *last* first date had been with my ex-fiancé over two years ago. The idea of dating still threw me into a panic.

"Since the DNA support group is on hold for the summer, Finn and I decided to meet and catch up."

At the last meeting, a woman had confessed to her husband that their son's upcoming DNA test results would reveal the man wasn't the boy's father. The meeting had quickly turned into an episode of *The Jerry Springer Show*. People were not grasping that the group's purpose was to share insights into DNA research and provide moral support to frustrated family historians.

Biddy rolled her eyes.

"You and Collin should join us for dinner, since you're not dating either. Just a dinner between friends."

Biddy's cheeks flushed pink. "That'd be grand."

Biddy had hooked up with her teenage crush, Collin Neil, after we'd helped him locate his brother Aidan and their family heirloom. Collin's grandma had insisted he attend the DNA support group meetings to learn more about his ancestry. The meetings had been the perfect cover for his and Biddy's *nonexistent* relationship.

Edmond held the back door while Rosie breezed out with a bright smile and three pies on a tray. She looked fully recovered from her confrontation with Pinky.

"Maggie would have been pleased with the turnout," Edmond said. He'd been sweet on Grandma before she'd passed. "Nearly a hundred former students plus guests. Same number of students that attended the school at any one time. Of course, many wouldn't have gone on a regular basis, as they'd needed to help in the fields or with chores at home."

"I had over five hundred kids in my graduating class. I can't imagine less than a quarter of that in this entire school. I've never attended my school reunion." It'd been five years since I'd seen my friends Caity and Melissa. After graduation I'd traveled the country and worked seasonal jobs, rarely spending time at my childhood home in a Chicago suburb. Growing up, I'd spent summers in Ireland hanging out with Biddy rather than bonding with friends back home at the beach or mall.

"Oh, I've been to a few of mine," Rosie said. "Not nearly as nice as this one. Maggie always did such a brilliant job. You're picking up right where she left off. She'd be so proud, especially with your memorial to her."

Edmond and I'd compiled photo boards of Grandma—from a young girl raised on the Flanagan homestead just up the road to the last photo of us before she passed at Christmas. Pictures illustrated the schoolhouse's transformation into a three-bedroom home in the early 1980s. The family photos included five generations of Flanagans, who'd attended school in my house. I smiled, tearing up.

The photographer, a middle-aged man dressed in jeans and a blue polo, gathered up people for the group photo. It never ceased to amaze me how he worked his magic, fitting two hundred people in front of my tiny yellow cottage. Yesterday, I'd replaced the dead flowers in the green window boxes with fresh perky ones. All the rain in Ireland couldn't give me a green thumb. Thankfully, Grandma's rosebush and the yellow daffodils that bloomed in spring were hardy and required little or no attention.

I assisted the photographer with positioning everyone, then went and stood next to Edmond and Rosie. I swore I saw a shadow move in my upstairs bedroom window. I did a double take, and it was gone. A comforting feeling wrapped around me. Grandma was there with me in spirit, watching over us.

After the photo, Mickey and a few others pulled out their fiddles, and people started dancing. No need to worry about anyone complaining to the guards, since all the neighbors were kicking up their heels in my backyard. It was going to be a fun, though long, night.

It was after eleven when everyone left. The kitchen mess wasn't going anywhere, so I'd leave it until the morning. Biddy had to work early, and I was exhausted from my pie-baking marathon and preparations for the reunion.

I trudged up the spiral staircase in the living room to put on my jammies. The office lamp cast light into the hallway. Odd. I was certain I'd shut off the lamp and closed the office door that morning. A drawer on the metal file cabinet was slightly ajar. The spines of several history and research books weren't flush with the others. The framed memorial card from Grandma's funeral sat on the opposite side of my scarred wooden desk.

The toilet in the master bathroom downstairs flushed.

Biddy hadn't left.

"Biddy!" I yelled, flying across the hall to check on my bedroom, where a full moon shone through a window in the slanted roof.

I flipped on the light. Clothes lay strewn across the green floral duvet on the double bed. Several perfume bottles were tipped over on the Irish lace covering the dresser top. Clothes spilled out of the drawers and onto the wooden floor. Exactly how I'd left the room that morning after flying around like a madwoman getting ready.

Biddy's flip-flops slapped against the stairsteps. She joined me in the doorway. "Janey! You've been robbed!"

I nodded, bolting back across the hall to my office. "Someone was in here."

Biddy's gaze darted between my bedroom and the office. "You think someone was rifling through *this* room, not your bedroom?"

"Everything is out of place." I pointed out all the evidence that someone had been in the room. I'd become very particular about keeping Grandma's office organized.

"Maybe a former student was looking for historical information on the schoolhouse and hadn't wanted to bother you when you were busy."

"None of the attendees would have gone through my stuff without asking. And I'm sure I had the door closed."

"If not an attendee, then who?"

I shrugged. "My grandma had over forty years of research in the file cabinet and boxes. I'd never be able to figure out what someone was looking for and might have taken. Not like she'd kept a client list. She was organized, yet kind of wasn't."

"Why would someone wait until now to steal research she'd done years ago? What about what you've been working on?"

"One client hasn't paid, so I haven't sent the research. Would be cheaper to pay the bill than to fly here from Australia and steal it." I collapsed onto the desk chair. "What if a thief snuck into the house while the party was going on, figuring nobody would notice? And nobody did?"

"Maybe someone was looking for hidden cash. Most of

the locals likely know we received part of the manuscript's advance. They might think we're rich."

After the Neil family's unpublished manuscript was featured on the TV show, it went into a bidding war. Collin's grandmother had insisted I take a 10 percent cut of the five-hundred-thousand-euro publishing advance. I'd split my share with Biddy. My twenty-five thousand euros—thirty thousand dollars—had gone in the bank. Biddy used a chunk to revamp her wardrobe and went down to working three days a week. In a funk over her job as a pediatric nurse, Biddy had jumped at the opportunity to reduce her hours due to the hospital's temporary cutbacks. If she didn't become more financially responsible, she'd be living behind McCarthy's pub and running the bar well into retirement.

"Janey! What if I'm next? Better call my mum and dad and warn them to sleep with the hurling stick by the bed. Crime is out of control here. Ya best be reporting it. Even if nothing of value was stolen."

"I have nothing of value except my lawn mower and..." I sprang from the chair and flew across the hall to my bedroom. I rifled through my underwear drawer for a small white box. I whipped off the top to find it empty. My stomach dropped. My only family heirloom was gone. Grandma's heart-shaped gold locket and key on a chain.

"Somebody stole my grandma's locket."

Biddy shook her head. "Oh man, here we go again."

Two

"ARE you sure the necklace was stolen and not merely misplaced?" Officer Negative Nellie's green-eyed gaze narrowed on my messy bedroom.

The middle-aged woman's sucky attitude hadn't improved since she'd ridiculed my Little Red Riding Hood theory when I'd been investigating Finn's car accident. However, my hunch had turned out correct—Finn's reference to the fairy tale during a coherent moment in the hospital had been referring to Gretta's *little red* car *hood riding* his car's bumper. The officer likely resented me for having cracked the case. This late at night, I'd assumed my 999 call would dispatch the Mullingar Garda rather than nearby Castleroche's, which kept limited hours.

"Yes, I'm sure. The locket is either on my neck or in that box hidden in the dresser drawer." I couldn't believe someone had been rifling through my undies.

"What's its estimated value?" Rather than poising her pen to jot down critical information, the officer flicked a white speck from her navy tie.

I shrugged. "I've never had it appraised. I doubt it's worth much money, but it has significant sentimental value."

Yet if the locket wasn't worth much, why had it intrigued appraiser Kiernan Moffat when I'd worn it to the *Rags to Riches Roadshow* filming? I'd been so focused on not screwing up in front of millions of viewers—possibly including my ex-fiancé—I hadn't questioned the shifty appraiser's reaction.

"The thief mightn't have had a clue if the necklace was worth two or two *thousand* quid," Biddy said. "Plenty of dumb thieves out there."

I placed a hand where the locket normally rested against my chest. Grandma had worn the necklace for sixty years after Grandpa's marriage proposal. I'd had it six *months*. I should have hidden it better. "It had my grandma's and grandpa's graduation photos." I stared at a framed photo of my grandparents on the dresser. "Might have been their only graduation ones..."

Biddy gave my shoulder a comforting squeeze. "I'm sure there are copies. Doesn't much matter since we're going to find the locket. We'll email the snap of it to every pawnshop in Ireland."

"Would you like me to email you the photo?" I asked the officer.

She nodded faintly, eyeing a framed genealogy print on my wall. *I'd rather find a dead man than a living one.* "That'd be grand."

Her lack of enthusiasm was far from reassuring.

The doorbell rang.

"Midnight booty call?" Biddy said.

The officer quirked a curious brow. More interested in my sex life, or lack of one, than my stolen locket.

"No. I have no clue who it is."

Hopefully, people didn't think my party was still going strong, since a dozen cars lined the road in front of my house. Those who'd had too much to drink had walked home or hitched rides with sober drivers.

I answered the door to find Biddy's mom, Ita, and several of the pub's regulars. Officer Negative Nellie's counterpart was out by the road smoking a cigarette, also taking my theft lightly.

"What are the guards doing here at nearly midnight?" Panic flickered in Ita's blue eyes. "Mattie was walking home from the pub and saw their car."

Mattie O'Toole trudged up the drive, red faced and huffing and puffing from trying to keep up with Ita, who ran several miles daily. Currently dressed in magenta-colored yoga pants and a gray T-shirt, she was prepared for an invigorating run at a moment's notice.

"Was a theft," I said.

"Jaysus." Mattie used his shirt sleeve to wipe sweat from his forehead. "Not yer new lawn mower, was it?"

I shook my head. "A necklace."

Mattie and the other two men let out relieved sighs.

"Your granny's locket?" Ita said.

I nodded, my eyes tearing up. Ita held out her arms, and I stepped down onto the stoop and into her comforting embrace. Biddy's parents were my second parents. Our moms had been friends. That was how Biddy and I'd met and became fast friends. After marrying and moving to Chicago, my mom had returned to Ireland less and less. Our moms had grown apart, whereas Biddy and I'd grown closer.

A vehicle came speeding down the road. I drew back from Ita and wiped away my tears. The officer and Biddy joined us as the driver slammed on the brakes and parked behind the row of cars. Tommy Lynch flew from his small truck, wearing a rugby team's blue jersey, red boxers, and green wellies.

"Not yer lawn mower or fuel, was it?" Tommy asked.

"Just a necklace," Mattie said.

"It wasn't merely a necklace," Ita scolded. "Was a family heirloom."

Tommy collapsed back against his truck in relief. "Johnny Gardner called on his way home from work that he'd seen the guards here. Good thing he didn't be waking Gretta. She barely sleeps as it is, hoping for something bad to be happening."

"You can all rest easy knowing it's not another yard thief," Ita said. "Now ya can be going home. Pub is closed for the evening."

"Best be sleeping with the hurling stick and hair spray next to the bed tonight," Biddy told her mom. "Just in case this wasn't a one-off occurrence."

The officer, Biddy, and I went back inside while the other officer lit up another smoke.

"Have there been any other home break-ins in the area?" I asked.

The officer shook her head. "Mostly theft rings nicking yokes from outbuildings and yards. Home thefts mainly involve cash and liquor. People are still not trusting the banks even years after the crash. I've been working double shifts due to the shortage of guards, yet no funding to be hiring more."

In other words, my insignificant family heirloom wasn't going to be a high priority over a theft ring.

"Ya might be wanting to ring Gretta Lynch about helping ya out. Did a brilliant bit of investigating helping us bust that Castleroche ring."

Suddenly Gretta was the area's supersleuth?

"Any of your reunion guests seem a bit suspicious?"

"Over two hundred people attended. My grandma held the reunion for forty years. Can't imagine someone robbing the house when everyone is always so thankful she'd continued the tradition. And now I am carrying on the reunions. Pretty much the same people every year. Yet I suppose the guests change, since spouses divorce or die and friends attend one year but not the next. I'll have a copy of the group photo in the morning. It's a tradition, and everyone who attends is in it. Anyone who *isn't* in the photo but was at the reunion would be even more of a suspect."

Biddy nodded. "Yet what's the chance a thief shows up the day of the reunion and uses that opportune time to rob ya?"

"Thieves cruise these roads looking for opportunities," the officer said. "They follow fuel trucks to know which tanks are being filled. Follow people from the bank and liquor stores, then raid their stash as soon as nobody's home. If a thief passes by a large gathering, he figures he can slip in and out of the house unnoticed, like pretending to use the loo."

The officer sounded convinced this was a random theft, if indeed a theft had even occurred and I hadn't misplaced the locket. As if a messy bedroom should make me an unreliable victim. Before she left, I promised to notify her if I discovered any clues from showing around the group photo. Like if anyone recalled a suspicious attendee or someone at the gathering who was missing from the photo.

"This doesn't feel like a random theft," I told Biddy. "What *thief* would rifle through research files?"

"A smart one. To make ya think he was searching for a file so you'd be focused on that for days before realizing your locket was missing. And might have thought you had a fiver hidden in each file."

I nodded. "Kiernan Moffat admired the necklace at the filming. What if he hired someone to steal it? He knew about the reunion. Gracie Neil mentioned it that day."

"He's certainly dodgy. Yet the woman who selected the lottery winners hadn't felt the locket was valuable or rare enough to warrant an appraisal."

Biddy's portrait of a butt-ugly woman had gotten us on the film set. Proving that the appraiser was far from competent at her job.

"The locket would have to be worth loads before a fella like Kiernan Moffat would risk getting caught nicking it," Biddy said. "Especially when he knows you're onto him."

Onto him about *what* we still weren't certain. We were just convinced he was a sketchy character involved in something illegal and had likely been Valerie Burke's partner in crime. Now that the woman—a descendant of Brenda Quigley—was in prison for insurance fraud and shooting Aiden Neil, had the appraiser moved on to his next scam to help support his expensive watch habit?

"We need to identify the thief and see if we can tie the

person to Kiernan Moffat. If I'd followed through on my instincts about his involvement in the Neil case, he might be in jail, and I might still have my locket."

Rosie's brother Albert, an antique dealer, had convinced me not to pursue my suspicions about Kiernan Moffat. Albert was a bit sketchy himself, having a reputation for purchasing and selling antiques with dubious pasts. He'd agreed that Kiernan Moffat was a shady character who'd managed to fly under the radar for years. Having had my fill of dodgy characters by that point, I was happy to allow someone else to expose him.

Now, I was questioning my decision.

Three

THREE O'CLOCK IN THE MORNING, I was lying in bed and staring through the skylight at the full moon. Merely a few hours earlier, someone had been in my bedroom rifling through my undies and personal belongings. The thief might have been searching inside my pillowcases and under my mattress. I squirmed against the cotton sheets. Trying to sleep in the master bedroom would be even worse. Grandma had been laid out on the bed for her wake. I needed to replace that mattress.

I grabbed my pillow and dragged my fleece blanket behind me down the stairs to the couch. I snuggled into the overstuffed red cushions and under the blanket.

What if the thief was out there right now stripping my grandparents' photos from the locket, preparing to sell it to a pawnshop? And some teenage girl bought it for selfies of her and her boyfriend? When they broke up, she'd whip the locket into the garbage, never to be seen again.

I had to find my locket!

I flew into the kitchen and filled a mug with steaming

water and two tea bags. I took my adrenaline fix and a baking tin with four pieces of strawberry-rhubarb pie into the living room. I plopped onto the couch in front of my laptop to devise a game plan. No email yet with the reunion photo. I'd sent the photographer a request three hours ago asking him to expedite it. Unlike me, he was probably sound asleep after a long day. Once I received the group photo, I'd question everyone in the area who'd attended. Someone had to have seen something suspicious or unusual. "Unusual" for this area didn't include an older man driving around in boxers and wellies in the middle of the night.

I compiled a list of pawnshops and jewelers within a fifty-mile radius, including Dublin. If I were a thief, I'd want to sell the evidence before the guards circulated a photo of it. Not that Officer Negative Nellie would be beating down doors to recover a low-value necklace I'd likely *misplaced*. Along with the photo, I offered a reward for information on the seller.

By seven o'clock I'd contacted over thirty shops when an email from the photographer popped into my inbox. It was an incredible shot, even with Pinky peeking out from behind an elderly man in the back row. The photographer assured me he could remove the photobombing sheep. Smiling, I replied the photo was perfect. After all, Pinky had attended and was becoming a permanent fixture of the schoolhouse. Who knew—his ancestors might have grazed in my yard back in the school days.

The photographer recommended a printing place in Mullingar. I was pulling into a nearby parking lot ten minutes before the shop opened when Edmond phoned.

"Heard ya had some excitement at your place after we left last night. Okay, are ya?"

"What'd you hear? That the stolen item was a diamond necklace I bought from the windfall I made on the Neils' manuscript? Or better yet, one I'd stolen from the Crown Jewels collection at the Tower of London back when I was an international cat burglar?" The story had had over ten hours to evolve into a wild tale.

"All I heard is that a theft occurred at your house, and 'twasn't your new riding lawn mower, fuel, hedge trimmer, chain saw, or power tools."

"Well, that's disappointing. My stolen locket isn't even a story worth embellishing."

"Maggie's locket?" Edmond muttered with concern.

I nodded, as if he could see me, fighting back tears. Like with Ita the night before, all it took was a few kind words from a loved one, and the tears started flowing.

"Ah-hunh," I managed between sobs.

"Ah, luv. Ring me later, will ya?"

I nodded again and disconnected the call. I sat in my car with my forehead on the steering wheel, crying until I got it out of my system, then headed over to the print shop.

While I was waiting, a text came through from my dad.

Tried calling yesterday. Need to talk to you about my trip to Ireland next month.

I hadn't noticed a missed call. Great. Dad was undoubtedly canceling his visit. What next? Since Mom's death almost four years ago, he'd thrown himself into his architectural work. His reliability rate had tanked. I'd text him later, unable to deal with one more issue right now.

Within a half hour, I was on my way home with a poster-size print of the reunion photo. When I pulled into my drive-way, there were still four cars parked out front on the road. If they weren't gone soon, the rumors would be flying that I was entertaining elderly gents at my home.

The rental company had picked up the picnic tables. Gretta Lynch had taped a note on the door offering to assist with my investigation. I was curious what story *she'd* heard.

Before I began questioning reunion attendees, I compared this year's picture with previous ones hanging on my office wall and in photo albums. Surprisingly, many of the same guests attended from year to year. So sad to think about the ones who'd passed away between reunions. Like Grandma.

Biddy was at work, so I was on my own. Not wanting people to think I was accusing them of stealing my necklace, I needed to be tactful and appear convinced that a thief had crashed the party. If someone suspected a local, the person would likely offer up the information.

There were few secrets in Ballycaffey.

The last time I was at Gretta's house with Biddy, Gretta had slammed the door in our faces. The time before that, she'd kicked Edmond and me out five minutes after serving tea. This time I'd been sitting on the cream-colored couch in her perky daffodil-yellow living room for a record fifteen minutes. We were drinking tea, eating ginger biscuits, and chatting about what a wonderful time we'd had at the reunion...until my locket was stolen.

Rather than her usual gray, Gretta was wearing a pink

blouse and tan slacks. "I should have insisted on remaining anonymous in that newspaper article. Criminals knowing my identity has blown my cover. Will make it more difficult to catch them."

Blown her cover? As if she were an international spy or undercover in a sting operation. Something told me that Gretta had found her calling and would be keeping Ballycaffey's roads clear of rubbish and robbers for years to come.

"If an attendee is the thief, my money is on Saddie Sullivan." She pointed out a smiley gray-haired woman wearing a blue dress. "According to Thomas, she hadn't attended school here but never misses a reunion. Was a blow-in from Sligo. Yet there she was at the gathering spooning potato salad straight into her purse. If she fancies something, she merely nicks it. Geraldine Smyth caught her walking off with her cat last week. Took the animal right from Geraldine's front yard, she did. And last month someone was visiting the woman's house and noticed birthday cards displayed on the mantel. Wasn't Saddie's birthday. She'd taken them straight from Charlotte Dougherty's postbox."

The entire town knew about the birthday card fiasco. Charlotte had confronted Saddie during the middle of Mass. The choir continued singing "I Will Raise You Up" while Charlotte took down Saddie in the aisle during communion. After hearing about the cat fight, Biddy and I vowed to attend church more often.

"The woman blames it on her sleeping medication, even in the middle of the day."

"Maybe she's a kleptomaniac and can't help it. Might have wandered into my house and taken the necklace without even realizing it."

I jotted down the woman's name but couldn't imagine she'd have rifled through my belongings in search of valuables. Sounded like if she saw something and the mood hit her, she took it. I suggested that rather than focusing on who was in the photo, we focus on who wasn't.

Gretta paced, tapping a finger against her thin lips. She came to a halt and spun around. "There was one fella I don't recall ever having seen before who's not in the snap. A short man in an oversized navy suit. He was about your height and around nine stones."

I was five foot three, not short for a woman, but a bit for a man. A stone was about fourteen pounds. Also, around the same weight as me.

"I remember thinking it was too warm for a suit, and he was a wee overdressed for the occasion."

"That's great." I perched on the edge of the couch and poised my pen on the notepad. "Do you remember any other details about him?" Being more of a visual person, I'd attempt to sketch the guy later despite possessing zero artistic skills.

"I wondered if maybe something had happened to his own suit, and not being from the area, he'd had to make do with what he found in a thrift shop. Even if he'd recently lost weight, the suit was still for a much taller man."

"Did he have any scars or identifying features?"

Like the missing sliver on my left eyebrow, which I penciled in for special occasions. A rogue flame from a baked Alaska had singed the fine hairs the summer I'd worked on an Alaskan cruise ship.

"If his jacket sleeves hadn't been cuffed, they'd have swallowed up his fingers, which were unusually fat for how thin he was. Though in all fairness to the fella, it was quite warm out. They might have been swollen from the heat. I noticed them because he held the door for me, which is the only time I recall seeing him. Doubt he was married. Couldn't imagine his wife allowing him out with the state of his outfit. He had a gold band on one of those chubby fingers, so possibly a widower."

In conclusion, I was looking for a short, thin widower with proper manners and freakishly fat fingers, wearing an oversized navy suit. As long as the man never changed his outfit, I might have a shot at catching him.

Rosie and Edmond were seated on the blue worn couch in his living room while I sat on a rocking chair. I'd removed stacks of genealogy and history books from the cocktail table to allow me to display the reunion photo. Last year's framed group photo hung crooked on the cracked white plaster walls.

"I should have worn my purple floral dress," Rosie mused.

"You looked perfectly lovely, as always," Edmond told her.

Her smile faded. "What's that on the front of it?"

"Must be a spot on the photo." Edmond shot me a panicked look.

I nodded, noticing the spot Rosie was referring to. Between the pie fiasco and having to quickly gather everyone for the photo, I hadn't spied the greenish-pink smear on the bottom of her dress.

Rosie gasped in horror. "It's pie filling." She glared at Pinky in the photo, her lips pursed.

"The photographer will be able to touch that up, no problem. He said it was even easy enough to remove the sheep."

Still giving Pinky the evil eye, Rosie said, "I certainly hope he's removing that animal from the snap."

I'd give Rosie a few weeks to cool down before telling her I planned to keep Pinky in the photo.

The woman's smile returned. "Everyone just raved about your grandma's strawberry-rhubarb pie recipe. You were so sweet to trust me with it."

"Of course. So do you recall seeing anyone there that isn't in the photo?"

Rosie studied the picture, brushing a finger over her strand of pearls. Edmond rubbed his chin in contemplation.

"Like maybe an older man..." I shouldn't lead a witness, but it seemed necessary. I'd polished off two cups of tea and four ginger biscuits while discussing the reunion and getting around to looking at the photo. At this rate I'd be hitting McCarthy's pub at closing time rather than before dinner-time—I'd intended to catch men on their way home from work.

Rosie's eyes widened. "Oh, my yes, a man in a bulky black suit. He refused a piece of strawberry-rhubarb pie. Who doesn't like pie? Must have been his first reunion, since all the past guests raved about Maggie's pies."

"Are you sure about the suit color?" Gretta had claimed it was navy.

Rosie nodded. "Most definitely black. The material

looked faded, as if it had been laundered in a machine rather than taken to the cleaners."

I perched on the edge of the chair. "Do you recall anything else about him?"

"He was short and quite thin. Much too small of a man for the suit."

At least the two women agreed the man was in desperate need of a proper-fitting suit.

"His jacket was missing a button. I was going to offer to sew one on. Maggie most certainly had a tin of odd buttons from over the years. Everyone does. It was a dark, medium-size button, nothing unique." Rosie shook her head. "I feel just awful for not having made the offer."

Edmond placed a comforting hand on Rosie's. "Don't be feeling bad, luv. You had a right bit going on helping out with the pies...and such..." He trailed off, avoiding the topic of Pinky.

She smiled faintly. "Suppose so."

"Also don't feel too bad, since he might be the one who stole my locket."

"Oh my," Rosie said. "A good thing I didn't be offering to hem his slacks. That really hadn't been an option. What would he have worn while he was waiting for me to finish?"

She appeared to be *waiting* for my answer, which I didn't have, so I peered over at Edmond. "Do you recall seeing this man?"

He shook his head. "Sorry. I don't, luv. But surely others must if Rosie does."

"Well, I only saw him the one time. He was inside heading toward the loo as I was going out with pie. It was at the time the photographer was collecting people for the photo. I remember thinking he'd better hurry up in the loo or he'd miss the group snap. Suppose he might have refused the pie because he hadn't wanted to take it to the loo..."

He had missed the photo on purpose. And rather than being in the loo, he'd been in my bedroom. It hadn't been Grandma's presence I'd thought I'd seen, and even felt, in my bedroom window during the photo. It'd been the shadow of the thief who'd stolen my family heirloom.

I stopped by McCarthy's pub in need of a cider ale and ibuprofen for my thumping headache. Too early for dinner after all the biscuits and scones I'd eaten that afternoon. Surely the men who'd attended the reunion would recall the mysterious man in the dark, ill-fitting suit. And they'd likely have been more focused on the man himself than his outfit.

A gold-lettered sign reading *McCarthy's* hung over the blue door of the small white pub. Inside, a crowd of men were shouting at two horses on TV sprinting neck and neck toward the finish line. A loud cheer erupted. Everyone took a celebratory drink. Biddy's dad, Daniel McCarthy—a tall, trim man—rang a bell behind the bar. He pushed up the sleeves of his green plaid button-up shirt, preparing to replenish drinks. He gave me a wave.

"How's the craic, Maggie Mae?" He pulled a pint of Guinness. He'd given me that nickname years ago, and it'd stuck. "Here to bet on the ponies, are ya?"

"I need to question a few people who were at the reunion. Didn't realize a race was on." The pub was packed with men who'd attended the event.

"Just ended. Now would be the time to grab 'em, as most bet on the winning horse." He gave me a wink.

I ordered a cider and circulated the crowd with the photo. After a half hour of coming up empty, I dropped onto a stool next to two reunion attendees. I bought the men a pint, and we became fast friends. I reminded the one gentleman to pick up his car still parked in front of my house before his wife came beating on my front door.

"Pie was grand, it was." The man's belly was stretching out a brown Jameson T-shirt and rolling over the waistband of his jeans. "Could ye be giving the recipe to me Betty?"

"Sorry. It's my grandma's secret recipe."

He frowned. "Right, then. Too bad."

"Party was great craic." The local barber was dressed in blue slacks and a white shirt. "Wouldn't consider having another, maybe come autumn?"

I shook my head. "Don't think so." Especially not the way this one had ended. I returned the conversation to the photo I had placed on the bar in front of them. "So anyone you recall having been there who isn't in the photo?"

The men studied the picture while enjoying their beer.

The barber rubbed a hand over his nearly bald head. "An older gentleman maybe...leaving when we were smoking in the drive."

"Aye." The Jameson man nodded. "A gray-haired fella in a dark suit, wasn't he now?"

I nodded eagerly, jotting down "gray hair." At least I knew the man wasn't bald.

"Had the bushiest eyebrows I'd ever seen," the barber said. "Should have offered to give them a proper trimming if he stopped by the shop."

"Do you recall the color of his eyes, shape of his nose, maybe a scar or mole..."

"The two of 'em were nearly one." The barber shook his head. "Never have I seen such eyebrows."

I took a huge gulp of cider.

"Had on a military ring." Jameson clasped his hands on top of his belly. "Noticed it because he was wiping sweat from his face. An older ring. Silver with a crown. Once worked with a fella from Antrim with the same ring. Figured the man was from the North, having been in the British military."

Had the man been wearing *two* rings—also a gold band, as Gretta had recalled? I was now looking for a short, thin man in a dark suit with bushy white eyebrows and a ring, maybe two, on his fat fingers. At least it would be easier to sketch a man without facial features.

Four

THE BALLYCAFFEY CEMETERY was located down a narrow rural road at the site of an abandoned medieval church. A massive wrought iron gate with spear-tipped posts allowed entrance through a towering stone wall covered with overgrown thorny bushes and hedges. The sun was sinking into the pinkish-blue sky on the horizon. I sat in my car in front of the gate, eating a double order of Kung Pao chicken and fried rice. My comfort food.

Besides compiling a detailed description of the possible thief's suit, the most productive part of my day had been Rosie's offer to forward the photo of my locket to her brother, Albert. The antique shop owner would likely agree to share the photo with other dealers. Out of the thirty pawnshops I'd contacted, eleven had responded that they hadn't bought or sold an identical locket.

Needing a few optimistic words of encouragement about my future, I cracked open the fortune cookie. No little slip of white paper was inside.

What the...cookie! No fortune? What did that mean? A

*mis*fortune cookie? Great. What a perfect time to get ripped off by my favorite takeaway place. Not to mention, I should have gotten two cookies for a double order. I crushed the cookie in my hand and flung the pieces out the car window. Several grateful blackbirds swooped in. I started the car, preparing to drive seven miles back to the restaurant and demand another cookie, maybe even a half dozen as backup!

Raindrops plopped against the windshield. I dropped back against the seat, a woman on the edge. A tiny meaning-less slip of paper was about to push me over it. *Get a grip.*

I took several calming breaths as I stepped from the car. Grandma would be proud to hear about all the compliments I'd received on her pies, and she'd tear up over the memorial to her. Hopefully, that would lessen the blow when I confessed that the gold locket and key—a reminder of her and Grandpa's eternal love for each other—had been stolen.

I blinked raindrops from my eyelashes and headed down the dirt path through the newer section toward my grandpar-ents' graves at the back. Grandma's and Grandpa's graves were near her parents and grandparents, where weathered gravestones and Celtic crosses covered in ivy and moss stood stoically on uneven ground. I left the path and traipsed through the tall grass covering a low sloping hill, touching my foot lightly on the ground before placing my weight on it. Tripping on a toppled-over tombstone or being sucked into a grave's sinkhole, like Biddy once had, would be the cherry on my day. Sixteen years later, Biddy was finally recovering from the traumatic incident, after entering a cemetery for the first time at Christmas.

As I neared my family plot, a dark figure came into view on the ground in front of my grandparents' gravestone. I cautiously approached the man in a dark suit lying motion-less on his stomach, facing away from me. A shovel lay on the ground at his side, next to a mound of freshly dug-up earth. Grandma having died merely six months ago, her plot's newly planted grass hadn't had time to catch up with all the green surrounding it, despite a wetter-than-usual winter.

The little hairs on the back of my neck told me to run like the wind. Instead I called out, "Excuse me. Can I help you?" *Dig up my grandparents' graves?* What a ridiculous thing to say.

The man didn't respond.

My heart thumped in my ears. I slowly stepped around to the man's front, and his vacant gray eyes stared back at me. I let out a squeal, stumbled backward, and fell onto my butt. I peeked back over at the dead stranger on my family's grave. Omigod. Had the elderly man suffered a heart attack while shoveling dirt?

He was short, thin, and had white bushy eyebrows. The bushiest ones that barber had ever seen. I couldn't tell if a button was missing from his dark suit jacket. His fingers were still wrapped around the wooden shovel handle—he wore a silver ring with a lion on one of his somewhat chubby fingers and a gold band on another...

The mysterious man in the dark suit from the reunion? What were the odds this wasn't the same man? It had to be him.

First my house was robbed, and now this man had attempted to rob my grandparents' graves.

With a trembling hand, I slipped my phone from my back jeans pocket. Before calling the guards, I phoned Biddy. It would take the police a half hour to get there, whereas

Biddy could be there in a matter of minutes. If I convinced her to come.

"Is this some kind of sick joke because ya think I was lying about being over my fear of graveyards?" Biddy said.

"As if I'd joke about a dead man on my grandparents' graves. He's likely the thief who stole my locket. His suit matches Gretta's and Rosie's descriptions, and his eyebrows are without a doubt the bushiest I've ever seen." I gasped. "I think his arm just moved," I lied. "What if he's not actually dead and there's a chance you could save his life?"

Biddy wasn't always rational, but she was ethical.

"Is there seriously a dead man on your grandparents' graves?"

"I'll send you the evidence." I snapped a shot of the man from the back and texted it to Biddy. When her phone didn't ding upon the photo's arrival, I checked my text. I'd sent it to Finn by mistake. Ugh. I texted it to Biddy.

"Janey Mac! Be right there!"

Biddy offered to call the guards while I phoned Gretta. Unlike Biddy, Gretta was excited at the prospect of a dead body on my family's plot. She hung up without a goodbye. If I called Rosie to identify the body, she'd bring Edmond, who'd likely have a stroke, and then I'd have two dead men on Grandma's grave. I took a picture of the man from the front, in case I needed it later, focusing on his suit rather than his eerie expression.

Finn replied to my text.

Fella had too many pints at the reunion, did he? Lol.

I doubted Finn would be "laughing out loud" when I told him it was a dead man on my grandparents' grave. Since that news was better delivered in a phone call than a text, I ignored his response. Sweating, I stripped off my denim jacket and stepped away from the grave, trying to get the pain in my chest and rapid breathing under control. I braced a hand on a leaning wrought iron fence surrounding three ivy-covered tombstones too weathered to read. Hugh and Eliza Cassidy. When I was young, I'd molded aluminum foil against the couple's headstone, enabling me to make out the worn letters. I'd also done several stone rubbings with crayons and large sheets of white paper.

A rustling noise startled me. I spun around to find the wind blowing through the leaves on a large oak tree.

I'd never been creeped out by a cemetery, until now.

Minutes later Biddy sprinted toward me in her pink Hello Kitty scrubs and purple tennies. I was having second thoughts about lying to get her here. If she was overcoming her trauma of cemeteries, this might seriously set back her recovery. Yet my heart raced, and my chest pain increased. I might need a nurse even more than a friend!

Biddy bent to check for a pulse and was startled by the man's open eyes staring at her. She glanced up at me. "As if you needed me to tell ya this fella's dead."

"I wanted to be sure. Besides, I need your moral support." I choked back several sobs and rubbed my chest.

Biddy gave me a sympathetic look and a hug. I hugged her back, not wanting to let go and face reality. She loosened her embrace and stepped back. "You're right. Sorry." She peered around the cemetery, scratching her neck, a nervous habit.

"What kind of sick person would dig up my grandma's grave?"

"Back in the eighteen hundreds, nicking dead bodies was

a huge source of income for grave robbers. They'd sell the bodies to the growing number of medical schools so students could—"

"La-la-la," I sang out, covering my ears.

Biddy slapped a hand away from my ear. "Fine. But you need to know how people protected their loved ones with inventions like grave guns, coffin torpedoes—"

"What if the person robbing the grave is killed?"

"That's the idea. The crime around here is out of control. Not enough guards to protect people. Lucky thing we have a brill community alert program."

"People might not have gone to prison for protecting the dead two centuries ago, but I'm sure I would now."

Biddy nodded. "A mortsafe might be the way to go. An iron grid that covers the grave. They were also used to keep the dead in, not just the living out."

"I highly doubt they still manufacture such a thing. Besides, I'm sure this man wasn't robbing the grave to donate my grandparents'..." My stomach tossed. "My house was just robbed, and now this guy shows up dead on my family's graves. It has to be the same man."

"Maybe he hadn't found what he was looking for in your house so figured it might have been buried with your granny. Coming across your locket might have merely been a bonus."

"As if my grandma would have been taking cash and valuables to her grave rather than spending it on the wake of the century or passing it on to family."

Biddy shrugged, then knelt next to the man. "Best check for your locket, if he was the thief."

"We shouldn't be tampering with a crime scene."

"What if the guards are stingy about sharing information with us? Besides, he's trespassing on *your* property."

Technically, my property was the two empty plots next to my grandparents. My mom was buried in Chicago, so they were now mine.

"A man's death likely trumps a trespassing violation," I said.

Biddy slipped a key ring from the man's jacket pocket, one lone key attached. "Cullen's Inn. If he was staying at a bed and breakfast, he obviously wasn't local and hadn't lived within a short driving distance."

Approaching sirens wailed in the distance. "Put that back in his pocket before the guards get here." I nibbled at my lower lip. "My necklace isn't in his other pocket, is it?"

Biddy checked and shook her head. My stomach dropped, and the sharp pain in my chest became more of an ache. I might never know what he'd done with my family heirloom.

She patted down his pants pockets. "No wallet, but another set of keys, likely for his car. Yet our cars are the only ones at the entrance."

A black streak flew through the cemetery gate and down the path toward us. Gretta. Instead of her usual gray attire and yellow reflective walking vest, a black cape was molded against her front and whipping in the wind behind her. Her long gray hair was out of its bun and slicked back with dark hair-color goop. She covered the distance of the cemetery in record time. Walking ten miles a day picking up road rubbish had given her great stamina and a trim figure. Maybe if I started collecting rotten food from ditches, I'd shed ten pounds. It would certainly curb my appetite.

Gretta blew past us and over to the deceased. After studying the body, mostly the suit, she smiled, not at all freaked out by the man's eerie expression. Had too many Irish wakes left the woman unaffected by the sight of a dead body?

She nodded. "It's indeed the fella from the reunion. Not only do I recognize his suit, but the gold band on his chubby finger."

Her ability to identify the man based on his outfit and ring were enough to satisfy me, but would it be enough evidence for the guards?

Biddy winced at Gretta's hair. "If it doesn't start lashing rain, ya need to be getting back to the salon and have that color washed out. You don't want it overprocessing." Biddy wasn't merely speaking as the daughter of a hairdresser, but from experience. Our attempt at coloring our own hair when we were thirteen had led to Biddy wearing her blond curly step-dancing wig for weeks to cover up her Bozo-orange-colored hair.

The deafening sirens and flashing blue lights stopped abruptly at the cemetery's entrance. Vehicle doors slammed shut. Officer Negative Nellie, her partner, and two additional officers dressed in blue with yellow garda reflective vests raced toward us. At least they were taking this crime more seriously than my stolen necklace. The man was likely the first dead person found on *top* of a grave in the Ballycaffey cemetery, so the Mullingar Garda had also been called in. Officer Negative Nellie joined us while the others checked out the body and blocked off the perimeter of my family plot with blue-and-white crime scene tape.

My grandparents' graves were officially a crime scene.

I swallowed the hard lump of emotion in my throat and blinked back tears. The officer's sympathetic expression and gentle green eyes were out of character as she had me recount my discovery. Maybe I'd have to start referring to Garda Doherty with a bit more respect.

"And I can confirm that man"—Gretta pointed a stern finger at the deceased—"was at the reunion the day of the crime. I encountered him exiting the back door at six twenty-three in the evening wearing precisely that same oversized suit and ring."

A bit dramatic, wasn't she?

The officer jotted down her statement, then peered expectantly at Gretta. "And?"

"It's without a doubt the same man."

"Based merely on his outfit?"

"And his gold band."

Biddy's gaze narrowed on Gretta's hair. "Ya need to be finding a spicket around here or get back to the salon to wash out your color. Seriously."

Biddy was becoming more concerned about Gretta's hair overprocessing than the dead body on my family plot. Maybe her Bozo-orange-hair incident had been more traumatic than her foot slipping into a grave.

Gretta nodded, handing the officer a card from her pocket. *Gretta Lynch, Investigative Services, Ballycaffey.* The woman had business cards? I didn't even have cards for my genealogy business.

An officer escorted Gretta and curious locals from the cemetery and sent away two arriving paramedics, no longer needed. An undertaker would now be transporting the body. The officer stood guard in front of the closed gate. Even if someone snuck past him, the person would have to scale the tall spear-tipped iron spindles to gain access. Not an easy feat unless you were properly motivated, like Biddy and I had been once when locked inside the cemetery.

The man's time of death was estimated as within the past one to two hours. If I'd arrived minutes earlier, I might have encountered the man digging up the grave and could have demanded answers to all the questions racing through my mind.

After the officer took my statement, Biddy and I watched the investigation from the other side of the blue-and-white crime scene tape a few graves over. The forensics team soon arrived. It was like an episode of *CSI*.

My phone dinged the arrival of a text. Finn. *The bloke is merely passed out, isn't he?*

I replied. Sorry. That pic was meant for Biddy.

That didn't answer his question and likely increased his curiosity. He called moments later. I turned off my phone.

Biddy eyed my cell. "Press already hounding ya for an interview, are they?"

"Finn. I accidentally sent him the photo instead of you."

Biddy grimaced. "What did he say?"

"I just texted him that the pic was meant for you."

She quirked a curious brow. "He wasn't at the top of your list of people to call upon finding a dead fella on your grandparents' graves?"

"I kind of have a lot going on right now, okay?"

Biddy shrugged.

My dad should also have been at the top of my list. If I told him what had happened, that would get him over here. But as upset as I was about him canceling or postponing his visit, I wanted him here when we could tour the country and have fun. Not now, when he'd insist I allow the police to do their job and stay out of the investigation. No way was I sitting back and doing nothing when there was a dead man on my grandparents' graves.

A forensics investigator slipped a purple item out from underneath the body. Biddy and I flew over to the crime scene tape. The man loosened the strings on the small purple pouch and peered inside it. An intrigued expression creased his brow, and he shared his discovery with the others. He nodded in my direction and handed the pouch to Garda Doherty.

What was inside the pouch?

The officer joined Biddy and me.

"What is it?" I craned my neck to peek inside the pouch from several feet away.

"The lab will have to analyze it, but forensics is quite confident the pouch contains remains. Especially considering it was found on a man digging up a grave."

"As in *human* remains?" Biddy took a step back.

The officer nodded. "Seen 'em before. Coarse like sand rather than light and flaky like cigarette ashes, as most people think."

Biddy's top lip curled back. "That's true. They're quite grainy. Remains once flew into my uncle Seamus's eye and scratched his cornea. Was a serious abrasion. He had to have surgery."

Poor Uncle Seamus had certainly had more than his share of bad luck. Kicked in the head by a donkey and having his cornea scratched by someone's remains. I had to stop whining about my streak of bad luck.

"Appears he was likely planning to *add* a body to the grave rather than steal one. Any idea whose remains these might be?"

I shook my head. "I've never seen that man in my life. Why would a stranger bury someone in my grandma's grave?"

"Because funeral and burial costs are mad these days," Biddy said. "My auntie Fiona couldn't even afford a wake. We had to buy tickets for a dinner cruise so we could toss her remains into the Irish Sea. Should have been tossing them straightaway after boarding instead of waiting until the end of the night, when everyone was ossified and not thinking clearly. Tossed them off the front of the boat, rather than the rear, and they flew back on *us*. Poor Uncle Seamus." She shook her head. "What's the world coming to when a person can't be holding a proper wake or burial?" Biddy's cheeks reddened with anger.

The officer stared at Biddy, undoubtedly searching for a response to her morbid tale. "Right, then." She returned our attention to the pouch. "But that's not all that's in here." She removed my locket dangling from her gloved finger.

Biddy and I gasped in horror.

"Told you it was stolen." I went to snatch up my missing heirloom, and the officer dropped it back into the pouch of remains.

My ears started ringing—either from Biddy's high-pitched squeal or because I was lightheaded and on the verge of fainting. I grasped Biddy's arm for support.

"Sorry. Can't be giving ya evidence. Might be finger-prints on it."

"Whose bloody fingerprints do ya think will be on it

besides Mags and that dead man's?" Biddy said. "Not like there'd be any fingers inside that pouch."

"It's protocol. And never know—the man might have had an accomplice."

Biddy's forehead scrunched. "If he'd had an accomplice, he'd certainly have insisted the person be here helping him dig up a grave so this guy wouldn't have a heart attack."

"Maybe the person *was* here. And can't be assuming the fella had a heart attack while digging the grave. Nobody here knew him or his health history. In the case of a sudden death and these circumstances, a postmortem will be performed."

"How else would he have died?" I asked.

The officer shrugged, a curious glint in her eyes. "Can't be making assumptions this early on in an investigation."

The hairs on the back of my neck again stood on end. "You think he might have been murdered?"

A man being murdered on my grandparents' graves would take this crime to a whole other level. And make me concerned for my own safety. Had I remembered to arm the security system when I'd left the house?

"There's no blood," I said.

"Foul play isn't always obvious," the officer replied.

Biddy nodded. "True. Could have been poisoned or injected with potassium chloride to make it look like a heart attack."

The officer quirked a curious brow.

"Saw that recently in a movie. And I'm a nurse. Or he might have been strangled with Mags's necklace."

I shot Biddy a horrified look.

"Of course, if he was strangled, he'd have bruises on his

neck." She glanced over at the officer. "Doesn't have bruises, does he?"

We'd been too busy analyzing the man's suit and searching him for evidence to look at his neck.

"I'm not at liberty to discuss."

"An accomplice would have taken the pouch," I said. "Who'd steal it, then bury it?"

Certainly not Kiernan Moffat. Looked like the appraiser was off the hook as an accomplice to the theft. He wouldn't have had the man dig up the grave and bury a *valuable* locket. Yet why had he been so intrigued by it?

"See, the man *was* robbing your home needing money to bury a loved one," Biddy said. "But the pawnshop offered him squat, so he was burying the evidence with the body, not wanting to get caught with it."

"Actually, that velvet pouch looks like a yoke you'd store jewelry in," the officer said. "The fella hadn't a clue he was going to die here. Maybe he'd planned to visit a pawnshop after the burial."

"Why would he have stored the locket with the remains?" I said.

The officer's gaze narrowed. "Maybe he'd nearly been caught red handed at your house, so he'd stashed the necklace in the only thing he had on him, this pouch."

"That still doesn't explain why he was burying remains in my grandma's grave."

"Might the person have been an unknown relation of yours?" the officer asked.

"Why wouldn't a relation ask permission to bury someone with my grandparents? Yet he'd taken time in the middle of the robbery to look at my grandma's framed memorial card."

"Might be how he knew she was recently deceased and buried here. Even if the forensics team rules this a nonsuspicious death and not a crime scene, outside of the deceased digging up your granny's grave, cause of death will still need to be determined. He'll be taken to the mortuary in Mullingar, and the postmortem will be performed in Tullamore." The officer stepped away and joined a conversation with the others.

Biddy discreetly slipped under the crime scene tape, plucked a strand of white hair from the dead man's head, and quickly scooted back over by me.

I smacked her arm. "Are you nuts?"

"The guards identifying the fella mightn't be telling us if he was your granny's rellie."

"Even if it's possible to get DNA from the hair, that tells us nothing unless he's in a criminal database to match it against."

Biddy and I exchanged hopeful looks.

Yet my gut told me I still needed to pay Kiernan Moffat a visit despite having hoped our paths would never cross again, especially not over some dead man on my family's grave plot.

Even if the appraiser didn't know anything about the theft, he knew something about my locket.

Five

THE FORENSICS TEAM ruled the man's death wasn't suspicious. Fingers crossed that the postmortem also ruled out foul play. Upon leaving the cemetery, I wanted to drive over to my former favorite Chinese takeaway place to demand a full refund and that they undo the bad luck their fortune-less cookie had contributed to my already crappy week. But a mile down the road, I pulled into the parking lot of Ballycaffey's recently reopened convenience store.

Needing to regroup, I took a calming breath while watching people come and go from the renovated store, which had suffered flood damage. A smiling woman walked out holding a to-go cup with a steaming beverage. Her young daughter tore the wrapper off a chocolate bar. Across the street, a man removed the sign from over the door at the former Casey's pub, preparing for the new owners' grand opening in two weeks. The pub had closed five years ago when the previous owner died. Biddy's parents weren't worried about the competition. McCarthy's pub was conveniently located for rural folks, and there was always room for one more pub in Ireland. Everyone was happy that Bally-caffey was coming back to life.

My phone rang. Finn. Undoubtedly checking to see why I hadn't returned his two voice mail messages I'd discovered upon turning my phone back on. I answered the call.

"Jaysus, Mags, can't believe ya text me that snap, then don't ring me back. Ya found that dead fella on your grand-parents' graves?"

"How did you know that?"

"Mickey rang my dad at the pub, who just rang me."

"The news already made it over to the pub in Drumcara?"

"Made it to me in Wexford, actually Clare." He let out a frustrated sigh. "Sorry. Just worried about ya. Are ya okay?"

"I'm fine." My tone was confident while I peered over my shoulder, making sure nobody was hiding in my backseat. I locked my car door. I filled him in on all the details and promised to keep him updated on any new discoveries. "Honestly, I'm doing okay. I'll see you in a few days."

"Sure you'll still be wanting to meet up?"

"Absolutely. And I invited Biddy and Collin to join us."

"Right, then. That's grand."

He didn't believe I was doing okay any more than I did, but he let it go and told me to keep him posted.

If Finn came over here, he'd try to keep me from investi-gating the crime, worried that someone might be after me or my locket again. No sense for us both to live in fear. When Gretta had knocked me out cold while I was searching for the person who'd run Finn off the road, he'd insisted I drop it. I had refused, and a major argument had led to him driving home to Wexford without even saying goodbye. Now, no way could I handle the added tension on top of dealing with the dead guy.

Besides, Finn hadn't offered to come over to protect me anyway. What was up with that?

I headed toward Edmond's to tell him what had happened before he heard it through Marjorie Walsh's rumor mill. Yet if the news had already reached Finn several counties away, Edmond had certainly heard some version of the story. Marjorie the Mouth spread gossip faster than Gretta's husband, Tommy, could slam a pint of Guinness. Precisely why it wasn't always accurate. By the time the news reached Edmond, it would be that Grandma's body had been dug up for a medical school's Anatomy 101 class. Yet I had to admit, I preferred Marjorie's grapevine over Tommy and Mattie's. At least hers gave an increased sense of importance and urgency to a rumor, whereas the men had downplayed the significance of my stolen locket, relieved that it hadn't been my lawn mower.

Fifteen minutes after I arrived at Edmond's, he was pouring a second whiskey, seriously disturbed by the news. "Just to be safe, maybe we should look into installing an alarm system or invisible electric fence around the graves that would zap trespassers and potential thieves."

Not quite as brutal as Biddy's grave gun or torpedo ideas, but still extreme for Edmond.

"I honestly think this was a onetime thing. The guy likely wasn't robbing the grave but rather adding...someone." A shiver crawled over me.

A faint smile curled the corners of Edmond's mouth. "Maggie would certainly have been intrigued by all this. She loved a good mystery."

I smiled. "That she did."

I pulled up the photo of the mystery man on my phone. Edmond plucked a pair of reading glasses from the breast pocket of his white button-down shirt and slipped them on. He studied the photo without batting an eye. People around here seriously needed to cut back on the number of wakes they attended. They were becoming immune to the sight of a dead body. Maybe if I'd sent the photo to Grandma's Irish niece, Angie, and a few other Flanagan relations, it wouldn't have bothered them one bit. But I'd wait until the police identified the man, then merely run his name by Grandma's rellies.

"If he was a relative of Maggie's, I'd never seen him before," Edmond said. "I agree with Biddy that the fella was possibly in your house looking for cash or valuables to fund a loved one's burial. Yet even if he came across Maggie's memorial card in your office and figured a recent grave could be easily dug up, would the man bury a loved one with a stranger?"

I shrugged. "Who knows? Some people are beyond cheap."

"He might have seen the necklace when you were on the telly and was a former antique dealer, so he knew its value."

The *Rags to Riches Roadshow* episode had been about recovering a family heirloom, so I'd mentioned the locket I was wearing. By doing so, had I invited a thief into my home?

"My grandpa certainly couldn't have afforded an expensive necklace. Yet maybe a thrift-shop find had become valuable over the past sixty years."

Edmond's gaze narrowed in confusion.

"What?" I asked.

He took a sip of whiskey, appearing to gather his thoughts. "Your grandmother once mentioned the locket is an heirloom, passed down through Liam's family. She commented that the key on the necklace symbolized more than merely the key to Liam's heart. She'd feared she'd said too much and quickly changed the subject."

Why hadn't Grandma told me the locket was an heirloom from Grandpa's family? We'd had numerous conversations about her parents having sold off any items of sentimental or historical significance outside of family photos. She must have realized the locket would have had an even greater meaning to me having been from Grandpa's family, which I knew nothing about. That made no sense.

Sitting in my car outside Edmond's, I was about to call Biddy when a text dinged. Dad.

Call Me Now!

His frustration came through loud and clear. Had the news about the dead body already made its way to *Florida*? How? Years ago, my parents had met when Dad's rugby team had played Ireland here in the Midlands. He hadn't stayed in touch with any Irish players or ever made friends here. On occasion he likely checked in with Biddy's parents to see how I was doing. They certainly wouldn't have called him about this without my approval.

Besides, he'd have been calling and not texting if he'd heard about the body.

I was too drained to deal with him canceling or postponing his trip indefinitely. I was holding on by a thread. I needed to keep it together and figure out why the mystery man was burying remains in my family's plot. I set an alarm reminder to call Dad tomorrow.

I phoned Biddy and recounted my conversation with Edmond.

"What if it's a key to a treasure chest?" Biddy said. "Or maybe to a drawer or safety deposit box that contains a *map* to a treasure chest?"

The gold key was the size of a peanut. "I don't think it's big enough to be a key to any of those."

"Maybe it's like in an adventure movie. When the archeologist fits an object into a hollow shape, a secret door slides opens."

"If the key has any other use besides being a lovely piece of jewelry, that man wouldn't have buried it."

"He mightn't have had a clue. I bet he planned to keep the pouch and necklace once he'd buried the remains. This reminds me of that Nancy Drew book—the one when Nancy tried on a jacket in a vintage clothing shop and found an old safe-deposit-box receipt in the pocket and a key sewn into the lining. She traced items from an old estate to local antique shops. It involved a missing will and a hidden fortune. Your Grandma might have been sitting on a *key* to a fortune and never known it. If she *had* known, she'd certainly have told you."

Would she have when she'd never mentioned the necklace was Grandpa's family heirloom? The only thing I possessed from my grandpa's past. A past I knew nothing about.

Something told me that was about to change.

Six

THE FOLLOWING MORNING, I dragged my butt out of
bed. I'd lain awake most of the night, staring through the
skylight at the full moon. Every time I'd closed my eyes, the
dead man's eerie gaze stared back at me. When I had finally
fallen asleep, I'd had nightmares about bodies lying on top of
graves rather than buried, the corpses grabbing for my feet as
I ran screaming from the cemetery. I could better understand
Biddy's trauma from her foot slipping into that grave.

Was the nightmare a sign that *I* was now afraid to step
foot in a cemetery? Heart thumping in my chest, I shoved the
disturbing thought from my head.

Despite being exhausted, I was anxious to solve *The
Mystery of the Person in the Purple Pouch*. However, Nancy
Drew certainly never had to investigate someone digging up
her grandparents' graves to *add* a body. Would have been a
bit morbid for the young adult series. My eagerness to solve
the case was impeded by having to shove the large dresser
from in front of my bedroom door. Finding a dead man,
possibly a murder victim, on my family plot had made me

paranoid and overly cautious. If the man had been murdered, what if his killer broke into my house looking for something else or thinking I had my locket back?

I made breakfast tea, grabbed a tin with the last two pieces of cherry pie, and plopped down on the couch with my laptop. I checked out the *Rags to Riches Roadshow* schedule. The show was currently filming at Russborough House, a stately home in County Wicklow. This was their final filming location before the summer break. The show wouldn't resume until fall. Biddy and I had to pay our appraiser friend, Kiernan Moffat, a visit within the next few days. First I needed to learn the dead man's identity in case there was still a remote chance he was somehow connected to the appraiser.

I wanted to know whether the man was possibly related to Grandma or Grandpa...and to me. After surfing the web for an hour, I came to the conclusion that the piece of hair Biddy had *acquired* from the man was useless without a follicle attached. Most DNA testing companies required at least ten to fifteen strands. Given a sufficient number of strands, one company claimed an 80 percent success rate in identifying a person's relationship to you for around two hundred bucks. Nail clippings had a 75 percent success rate. You could also test dental floss, cigarette butts, and other items that made my skin crawl. There were specific DNA tests for identifying grandparents, paternity, siblings, and aunts or uncles. The closest relationship the elderly man could have been of mine was a great-uncle, an unknown sibling of Grandma's or Grandpa's.

I shot the company an email inquiring about the possibility of testing more distant relations. If they had the capability of providing a raw DNA file—the DNA extracted from the sample—to upload to genealogy research sites, they'd certainly be advertising it. I asked my social media genealogy groups if they knew of a company that offered this service.

DNA testing was rapidly evolving. What couldn't be tested today might easily be tested tomorrow.

I wasn't certain how I felt about conducting a DNA test on a dead stranger without his consent. Yet how ethical was it for the guy to have been digging up my grandma's grave even if his intention was to "donate" to it rather than robbing it?

Continuing to Google DNA sites, I came across one that tested remains. How in the world could they extract DNA from remains with the consistency of gritty sand? I shuddered at the thought of poor Uncle Seamus's eye. At least the company had a disclaimer in bold stating the chances of a successful DNA extraction was quite low. Less than 1 percent was my guess. Hopefully, I wouldn't become desperate enough to drop several hundred bucks on a test with almost zero chance of return.

The doorbell rang, startling me.

I stepped cautiously into the mudroom. The view through the green door's small window was obstructed by the large red coatrack with jackets and umbrellas hanging from pegs. Another security measure. I pushed the rack aside to find the two elderly ladies who'd brought me meals after Grandma's death. They'd taken that opportunity to voice their opinions about selling the former schoolhouse to strangers from outside the townland.

I opened the door, and the scent of potatoes and a red meat sauce filled my nose. Shepherd's pie. My stomach growled with delight, recalling how delicious their dish had been the last time. Surprisingly, it'd been made with beef rather than the traditional lamb. When I was ten, my mother insisted I try lamb. The gamey taste and smell had made me throw up. Not a pretty memory.

The lady with a brown tightly curled wig handed me the foil-covered glass dish, giving my coatrack a curious look. "We think ye did the right thing, luv."

"Would have done it meself." The white-haired woman gave me a sympathetic smile. "Need to be protecting our loved ones, we do. Dead or alive. What's the world coming to when ye can't even rest in peace having to be worrying about yer body being nicked."

"If ye don't have a plot yerself, there's sure to be a sale on 'em now, with the graveyard's reputation and all. They'll be wanting to ensure future burials."

"I already have one," I said. "Two, actually."

"Oh, that's grand, isn't it now?" the wig lady said. "Such a young lass thinking ahead to the future rather than merely living in the moment, like so many nowadays."

Her friend nodded. "But if ye know anyone in need of a resting place, Emma Donavan is auctioning off her site at bingo tonight. Expected to go for at least twenty-five percent less than what she'd paid. It's on the far west side with plenty of sun exposure. A premium spot. Even though I wouldn't want to be laid to rest next to her husband. A crotchety old man, he was."

"Not like you'd be having to listen to him," her friend said.

"Suppose not. Might be worth the view."

They left me there holding the dish, wondering exactly

what the conversation had been about. *They would have done the same thing?* They headed down the drive, passing Gretta walking up it. The ladies shot horrified glances over their shoulders at Gretta's pitch-black hair—a few shades darker than my blacktop drive. I tried to avoid staring at her over-processed hair color and asking if she'd like to borrow Biddy's curly blond step-dancing wig.

"Wanted to let ya know, I'm patrolling the area around the graveyard, keeping an eye on things. Needless to say, everyone is a bit concerned about their loved ones there." She flipped her hair over her shoulder.

I nodded. "Great idea."

"Johnny Regan was sacked after having run over many of the graves' decorations due to his failing eyesight and refusal to wear proper glasses. I offered to take over as temporary caretaker as part of my required community service hours. If you should need any assistance, though, I'm sure I could find the time." She tucked a few strands of hair behind her ear.

Was she drawing attention to her hair, fishing for a compliment?

"I could show the fella's snap around and see if anyone recognizes him."

Thankfully, I hadn't emailed her the picture. I didn't want to be responsible if she approached someone who *wasn't* unaffected by the sight of a dead body.

"Thanks. I'll let you know."

Gretta left with a disappointed look—I hadn't offered a research task and hadn't complimented her hair. However, she'd given me a great, kind of creepy, idea.

I downloaded the mysterious dead man's photo onto my laptop and then uploaded it to Google Images. Maybe the search engine would find similar photos on the web. Like the man's profile picture on Facebook or a photo of him in his church newsletter. Most images that came up were men in dark suits or ones with a similar shocked and eerie expression. Like an ad with a man freakin' out over an outrageous cable bill. The search homed in on one object, like the suit, more so than people who resembled the person himself.

I shut down my computer.

I had several genealogy clients waiting for me to retrieve copies of wills and probate records from the National Archives of Ireland in Dublin. Locating wills was hit or miss. Most of them from the seventeenth through the nineteenth centuries were destroyed in the Public Records Office fire in 1922 during the Irish Civil War. After that as many copies as possible were collected from solicitors' offices and other depositories.

I should have spent today in Dublin rather than going stir crazy accomplishing nothing, but I couldn't have focused. I emailed the clients I'd hoped to get back to this week and informed them that my research was delayed due to extreme personal circumstances. I offered them a 50 percent discount for the inconvenience. Better to take a financial hit than to be dinged by bad reviews on Google or social media, as my business was just taking off.

Besides avoiding work, I was avoiding the cemetery and checking on my grandparents' graves. I needed to fill in the hole if the guards hadn't. I *needed* to face my fear. My career as a genealogist was doomed if entering a cemetery brought on a panic attack rather than an exhilarating sense of adventure over what I might discover. My discovery preferably being a tombstone that helped solve a ninety-year-old family mystery rather than a corpse of a ninety-year-old dead man.

After devouring two servings of the delicious shepherd's pie, I triple-checked that the security system was armed and headed out. A half mile down the road, I turned around and drove home. I opened the front door and waited for the alarm's frantic siren to calm my nerves and OCD. Dogs barked, sheep baaed, and cows mooed from a mile away. Pinky pushed himself up from the grass and trotted off to find a peaceful spot to sleep. If it went off one more time, I'd have the guards at my door.

Hmm... That was one way to get Garda Doherty's attention. I'd left the officer several voice mail messages inquiring about the dead man's identity and his autopsy date. I hated being in limbo and afraid of another attempted robbery. I debated driving over to Cullen's B & B to see what I could learn about their recent guest. However, the only way I knew where the man had been staying was that Biddy had tampered with a dead body. If my visit to the B & B got back to the guards, the officer might not hesitate to file charges against us. Despite having been sympathetic about me finding a dead body, she was likely still itching for a reason to arrest me and keep me out of her hair.

On my way to the cemetery, my phone's alarm rang out in my purse, reminding me to call Dad. The annoying noise continued for another mile until I arrived at the cemetery's gate. I turned off the alarm, took a deep breath, and called him.

"I've been worried sick that you haven't returned my call or texts," he said. "Planned on calling the McCarthys today if I hadn't heard from you by noon."

He'd have been a lot more worried if I *had* called and told him everything that had happened the past two days.

"Sorry. So you're not coming for a visit?"

"Yes, I'm coming, just not in August. I received an invite for a Murray reunion in September. The first one they've ever held, as far as I know. I'd like to move my trip back so I can go from Ireland to Edinburgh for the gathering. Thought you might be interested in going with me."

A handful of DNA support group members, Dad, Biddy's family, Edmond, and Finn were the only people who knew my dad wasn't my biological father. Neither my sisters, Emma and Mia, nor any of Dad's family knew. Thankfully, Dad was more into *living* relations than *dead* ones. If I'd traced his tree back ten generations only to later learn I wasn't a Murray, it would have made my DNA discovery even more devastating.

"If you don't want to go, I understand," he said.

Did I want to go?

"Honestly, it's okay if you're unable to attend." His usual easygoing tone filled with disappointment. "Your sisters have no interest in it."

Big surprise. If a major finance conference was being held there, Emma and her husband, Dread Ted, would have been all over it. Mia had dropped nearly ten grand on a state-of-the-art double convection oven, yet she wouldn't spend two thousand on a family trip to Scotland. They probably thought I'd be going.

"Is it okay if I move my trip back three weeks?" he asked.

"Of course. And of course I'd like to go with you to the reunion." Wouldn't I?

Then why was my heart racing out of control?

Dad's grandparents had emigrated from Scotland shortly after they married, so most of his relatives were still there. His parents had passed away when I was in high school. Three cousins had visited us in Chicago a few times, but Dad hadn't been to Scotland. The Scottish men were a total riot and always brought us gifts. I still had the small stuffed sheep in a kilt and the customized T-shirt that read *Lady Mags Murray*. Sadly, the shirt was now too small.

"Take a few days to think about it," he said. "I have to send a reply next week."

"Okay." Did I need to think about it?

When I called him in a few days, my life would be back to normal. I would have solved the mystery of the man with the purple pouch and could fill Dad in on all the details rather than worrying him now. And I could think more clearly as to why the thought of attending the reunion had me on the verge of a panic attack.

It wasn't because I'd see my sisters, since they weren't going. When I'd decided not to sell Grandma's house and share the sale of what was rightfully mine, Mia had stopped emailing me recipes I never made. Emma no longer asked me to take pictures of filming locations for *Game of Thrones*, filmed in Northern Ireland three to four hours from my house.

It had been a peaceful six months.

I arrived at the cemetery and let out a relieved sigh that Gretta was nowhere in sight. She must have taken a late lunch. I didn't feel like chatting or having her hover over me while I planted the purple pansies I'd uprooted from my window box to plant on Grandma's grave. I was also thankful that pulling up in front of the cemetery's gate hadn't instantly triggered traumatic flashbacks of yesterday.

I focused on happy memories to block out my nightmare of corpses grabbing my feet. Like how Grandma had organized scavenger hunts to keep me occupied while she was conducting research. Finding the grave with the earliest death or most interesting name...

At that time, there were twenty-four Margarets-slash-Maggies buried here. Paddy O'Toole was the most Irish-sounding name. Aoife, Eabha, Meabh... All the traditional Irish girls' names I had no clue how to pronounce. Grandma would then teach me how to say them. Hugh and Eliza Cassidy died in 1762. The oldest grave in the cemetery. I'd spent several hours molding aluminum foil against all the weathered tombstones, enabling me to transcribe them. Our game had also assisted Grandma, who was transcribing the Ballycaffey cemetery at that time. I'd become a genealogist at the age of nine without even knowing it.

Now, here I was standing in front of my grandparents' graves, smiling, not the least bit panicked. Well, maybe a little, but that was to be expected. I wasn't immune to the sight of a dead body, like Gretta, Edmond, and Biddy. The blue-and-white crime scene tape was gone from around the perimeter of my family plot. However, the pile of earth the man had dug up was still there. While planting the perky flowers in the hole, I assured my grandparents, and myself, there was no need to worry about anyone else attempting to dig up their graves. This had been a onetime occurrence. And as soon as I learned the man's identity, I'd give them an update. I patted down the soil, still moist from a recent shower.

I sat at the foot of my grandparents' graves, squinting back the sun, peering around the peaceful cemetery. A sense of comfort washed over me. Feeling Zen, I lay back on the cushiony long grass and closed my eyes...

Loud voices and a sharp pain in my chest woke me from a peaceful sleep. Was I having another panic attack? My eyes shot open, squinting back sunlight, to find Gretta arguing with two teenage boys. One of them held a stick hovering over my chest. Likely the cause of my pain.

"Delete the snaps," Gretta demanded.

The tall dark-haired guy held his phone up out of the woman's reach. "We found the body first. Had merely been wanting a snap of the grave where the robber was killed to show the lads at the pub. Another dead body is bloody brilliant."

Another dead body?

"'Twasn't robbed," Gretta said. "A fella died here while visiting the grave. So don't be spreading those rumors. And this woman's not dead. If ya don't be deleting those photos, I'll be calling the guards."

"Grand. They'll be wanting to know about the body," said the short blond guy in a Jameson shirt, holding a Guinness beer.

"And the cemetery is a public place," the other said.

"Actually, I own the plot you're standing on," I said.

The boys' panicked gazes darted to me.

"Jaysus." The Guinness can slipped from the blond guy's hand and landed on my leg, soaking through my jeans.

"See"—Gretta gestured to me—"she's not dead. Was merely sleeping."

"Wasn't sleeping," the Guinness guy said. "I poked her a half dozen times. She didn't move a bit."

Because she'd barely slept a wink last night.

"Delete the photos, or I'll haunt you to your grave," I said in an eerie voice.

The tall guy deleted the photos while Gretta watched, and his buddy took off running toward the front gate. Once the photos were gone, so was the guy.

Gretta shook her head. "Lads are ossified. However, can't say I entirely blame them. Was afraid myself you might be dead, lying there so still, looking so peaceful. But I figured, what was the chance of two deaths taking place on the same grave in a matter of days." She took a calming breath. "Scared the daylights out of me, ya did."

It was good to know the thought of my death concerned Gretta rather than making her happy to have another mystery to solve. It was even better to confirm that I was relaxed enough to fall into a deep sleep in a cemetery instead of running scared from one. If the dead man did have an accomplice, why would the person return here when the cemetery was now on the guards' radar, and, more importantly, the locals'?

"It's been quiet today outside of those lads." Gretta frowned at the surroundings.

"What time is it?"

"Half five. I'll be here a few more hours."

I thanked the woman for being so vigilant in watching

over the cemetery and setting those guys straight. With my luck lately, their photo of me on the grave would have gone viral on social media.

Rather than my sisters calling Biddy to verify my death, they'd be calling a real estate agent to have my house put on the market tomorrow. I needed to download an online template for a will and designate Biddy as the beneficiary of my home!

Seven

I HEADED to McCarthy's for a pizza and cider. When I entered the pub, two older men playing darts raised their pints to me and told Ita to pour me one. The men looked like brothers. Both were short and stocky with receding gray hairlines. One always wore soccer jerseys, the other John Deere T-shirts. The regulars had never bought me a beer before.

"What's that about?" I asked Ita.

She grabbed a bottle of cider from the small fridge behind the bar. "Story is that you hit the fella over the head with a shovel, killing him after catching him digging up your granny's grave."

"What? If I'd killed him, I'd be in jail, not a pub."

And here I'd been worried about my safety if the guy was murdered, when I should have been more concerned about the Ballycaffey rumor mill. It was also good to know that Gretta had attempted to squelch those two guys' rumors of a man having been killed rather than feeding into the gossip. That was obviously what those two little old ladies had been commending me on, assuring me they'd have done the same. They'd been quite heated over the thought of a grave robber digging up their loved ones. I could see them knocking off a thief with a glass dish of shepherd's pie.

Biddy entered through the residence door behind the bar, dressed in Scooby-Doo scrubs. "Ah, there she is. The Shovel Slayer. Against using a grave gun or coffin torpedo, but a shovel is just grand, is it?"

"Is that what they're calling me?"

Biddy shrugged, sliding onto a stool next to me. "Haven't a clue, but it's what I'm calling ya. Unless ya fancy Cemetery Slayer better."

"I don't fancy any nickname. I don't want this story getting around and influencing the pathologist's report."

Yet my stomach gurgled at the thought of more women dropping off comfort food.

"I think a cracked skull will be influencing the pathologist's report rather than Marjorie Walsh's gossip minions."

"What if he ended up with head trauma from falling on the ground?"

"Did you touch the shovel or the body?"

"Of course not."

"Then you're grand."

"But you touched his keys."

"Janey," Biddy muttered. "I did, didn't I?"

"What were ya doing digging through a dead man's pockets?" Ita demanded.

Biddy was saved from having to respond when a group of rowdy guys entered the pub and Ita went over to serve them.

"I did a bit of research today," I said. "That strand of hair can't be tested without a follicle intact. And companies require ten to fifteen strands."

Biddy slouched in disappointment. "Any other options?"

I pulled up the DNA testing website on my phone.

Biddy scanned it, her forehead crinkling. "How are ya supposed to be getting earwax from a person without him realizing it?" Her top lip curled back. "Don't even get me started on some of those other samples." She glanced at her mom pouring pints. "Would ya be able to do that poor fella's hair for the wake?"

"Why's the wake being held here if the man wasn't local?" Ita asked. "Hasn't yet been identified, has he?"

"Doesn't matter if he's local when he might be Mags's rellie. And we'll be needing fifteen strands of hair."

"For what?"

Biddy explained our DNA mission.

Ita shook her head. "I'll be doing no such thing. Not ethical, it isn't."

"As if there's a hairstylist code of ethics."

"Doesn't need to be. A person naturally has 'em."

Biddy looked offended by her mom insinuating she lacked a moral compass. "Fine. I'm sure I'll have no problem getting them on my own."

Ita shook a stern finger at her daughter. "Stay away from the man's hair. Make that his entire body. Don't need to be bailing ya out of jail for tampering with a corpse. Would never be hearing the end of it at the salon."

"Guess you don't be wanting in on the treasure Mags has a key to."

Ita gave her a curt nod. "That's right. Wouldn't be

wanting any part of your crazy plan." She glanced over at me. "And you'd be best not to either."

"Mags has plenty of her own crazy ideas. She doesn't be needing mine. Although it's totally brill."

Garda Doherty entered the pub. Several patrons set down their pints and started chatting, overly nonchalant. One man slipped out the side door before the officer looked his way. I'd have to remember to ask Biddy what that was about.

"Not here to be arresting the lass, are ye?" The man in the green soccer jersey turned from his game, dart in hand midair.

"Self-defense, it was," his friend said.

The officer's gaze narrowed in confusion. "What lass?"

Besides Ita bartending, Biddy and I were the only lasses in the place. Biddy tensed, and I held my breath.

"Oh, ah, right, then," the man stammered, lowering the dart. "A lass was in here earlier, and she, er..."

"Forgot to leave quid for her pint," his John Deere friend added, nodding too eagerly. "We covered it. No need to be tracking her down."

"How was that self-defense?" the officer asked.

"Who'd be saying anything about self-defense?" The John Deere guy peered innocently at his buddy, both men shrugging. "Just wanted to be helping out. Know how busy ye are investigating the murder."

The officer's expression relaxed. "We haven't confirmed foul play, but thanks a mil for your concern over our workload."

The men smiled proudly and went back to their game of darts. Biddy and I let out relieved sighs.

The officer joined us. "Lab results show the pouch indeed contains remains. Also identified the deceased as Duncan MacDonald from the Isle of Bute, Scotland. Came over on a ferry with his car. Found the vehicle up the way from the cemetery."

My eyes slowly widened. "Isle of Bute."

She raised a curious brow. "Know someone from that area, do ya?"

I shrugged. "My grandpa's family might have been from there. But his last name was Fitzsimmons, or maybe Collings."

The officer's gaze narrowed. *How didn't I know my own grandfather's surname?*

Good question.

"I was only four when my grandpa died."

And why wouldn't Grandpa's surname have been the same as my recently deceased Grandma's?

I'd questioned the truth about Grandpa's last name after discovering that a fairly close DNA match, Simon Reese, had a grandmother, Eleanor Fitzsimmons, born on the Isle of Bute. I'd found a baptismal record for a Henry *Collings* born on the island the same date as Grandpa, but no Henry Fitzsimmons. Grandpa's full name was Henry Liam Drummond Fitzsimmons. He'd gone by Liam. The fact that the mother's surname on the birth record was Drummond also led me to believe it might be Grandpa.

"So the man must be connected to your grandpa, not your granny," Biddy said. "Would make sense that he decided to dig up the dirt of a fresh grave rather than your grandpa's, with loads of grass and weeds. Probably thought with so little grass on her grave, ya wouldn't even notice a small hole filled in."

"Interestingly, the fella registered at the B and B as Dougal McGuire, whereas the name on his passport and driver's license was Duncan MacDonald." The officer eyed me. "A bit odd, wouldn't you say, two different names?"

I nodded.

"Dougal McGuire sounds familiar," Biddy mused.

"Could your grandfather's last name possibly have been MacDonald or McGuire?"

"No," I assured her. Yet it very well could have been, for all I knew. "Was he staying in the area?"

"Over the New Delvin way."

The location narrowed it down to a handful of bed and breakfasts, making it less suspicious should the officer discover we'd been snooping around at Cullen's B & B.

"Someone is coming from Scotland tomorrow to identify the body. The postmortem is set for the following morning. If all goes well, the body should be returned to Scotland by the end of next week."

Only two more days of pushing furniture in front of doors, triple-checking the security system, and being called the Shovel Slayer. Unless the autopsy concluded the man had been murdered. Then what was I going to do?

"Wasn't any head trauma, was there?" Biddy asked. "Like from a hard object..."

I glared at Biddy.

Everyone's concern for my welfare and innocence was going to end up getting me life in prison!

The officer shrugged. "Postmortem will tell."

"Hopefully his relative can explain the reason for two different names." I brought the topic back on track.

"Not a relation. A Presbyterian minister is identifying the body. Fella had no known family."

"How sad is that?" Biddy frowned. "Likely why the poor fella had to travel to Ireland to bury the body, if he's related to your grandpa. We need to hold a wake. One more sign we should be starting our business—Fake Your Wake." Biddy turned to the officer, inspiration flashing in her eyes. "Holding a wake while you're still alive is a brilliant way to learn who really cares about you, don't ya think? Then you'd know who to cut out of your will and who to leave in. Weed out the ungrateful eejits *before* ya die. Our slogan will be *Legit or Eejit*. Is that totally brill or what?"

"I don't have a will," the officer said.

"I can't afford to hold a wake for someone I didn't know," I said.

"Might not have known him, but you're likely related to him," Biddy said. "It only seems right to fulfill his dying wish and give the person in the purple pouch a proper burial. After all, the fella died on your property."

"While committing a crime," I said.

"This is a bit of a unique situation." The officer's gaze narrowed. "Not sure what will be happening with the remains. Will have to ask the sergeant."

"The person at least needs a proper urn," Biddy said. "My auntie Violet has a bronze pet urn. A statue of a cow. Seamus bought it at a thrift shop, thinking it was a doorstop."

I didn't want to ask if the urn was empty. Or if it was

common to have a pet cow cremated in Ireland and its remains displayed on the fireplace mantel.

Before leaving, the officer promised to contact me tomorrow about when my locket would be released from evidence. The second the door closed behind Garda Doherty, everyone grabbed their pints to resume drinking, including me.

"We really need to come up with a proper name rather than calling it the person in the purple pouch. After all, it might be your rellie."

I nodded. "How about Nancy Drew? This whole thing reminded us of a book from the series. The name Nancy covers the person if it's a woman, Drew if it's a man."

Biddy smiled. "Ah, that's grand, it is."

We clinked glasses and drank to our brilliance.

"We need to hang around outside the mortuary and meet that minister fella, offer him some moral support when iden- tifying the body," Biddy said.

"You're *not* snagging that dead man's hair in front of a minister. He'd likely find tampering with a dead body irrever- ent, not to mention just plain creepy."

"Of course not. You'll need to be distracting him so he doesn't notice me acquiring DNA evidence."

"According to members on my forums, no company would be capable of providing the man's raw DNA file to upload to genealogy research sites and compare to DNA matches. It might be a week, month, or years before that technology is available."

"Loads of cold cases are always getting solved years later using DNA. It must survive a long time."

"I don't want to wait years to figure this out. Maybe it's

an elderly minister who knew this Duncan MacDonald's background and possibly my grandpa's."

"And if he doesn't know much about either, we'll have to make a road trip to the Isle of Bute. Offer our assistance with the wake since we're quite experienced in that area." Biddy gasped. "We should also offer to help clean out the fella's house so we can check under the mattress, the back of picture frames—all the usual hiding spots for secret information. If nothing else, we might score some cash. Like the guard said, many elderly are still hiding money in their homes. That would help pay for the wake and his burial. If you're his only relation, the rest is rightfully yours."

I had the feeling this whole thing was going to end up costing me way more than I'd be making.

☘ ☘

Once home, I called Edmond to give him an update on the deceased, Duncan MacDonald, from the Isle of Bute. I was also curious if he'd heard the Shovel Slayer rumors circulating about me.

"Shovel Slayer? Don't recall hearing that one."

He was as bad a liar as the men at the pub. "What nickname *do* you recall hearing?"

"Actually, didn't hear a name, just that you'd smashed a broken tombstone slab over the fella's head."

"Next thing you know, I'll have had an adrenaline rush while heaving my grandparents' tombstone from the ground and crushing the man with it."

"That would be a brilliant tale, but ya probably don't want me to be spreading it."

I told him about the garda having identified the dead man. "Do you recall my grandpa ever visiting that island or Scotland?"

"No. He did on occasion travel to Belfast to visit someone. Suppose he might have been taking a ferry across to Scotland."

I might be taking that ferry myself in the near future.

I promised to keep Edmond posted on any developments.

I'd always dreamed of visiting Scotland. The Murray Clan of Atholl was from the Scottish Highlands. The clan's tartan was a lovely blue and green—very Irish looking. Good thing, since my DNA showed I wasn't the slightest bit Scottish. After years of attending the Scottish Highlands Games in Illinois, I'd acquired numerous items designed in the Murray tartan. Wool scarves, pins, and even a wool cap that I only wore to the games. It might be a good idea to wear one of my Murray Clan T-shirts tomorrow when I met the minister, to give us a Scottish connection. It wasn't like I'd be lying to a minister. Even though I didn't have Scottish DNA, Scotland and the Murray Clan would always be a part of me.

So, why hadn't I yet called my dad and confirmed my attendance at the Murray reunion?

Did I feel I'd have to be honest about not being biologically a Murray? That I was a fake? It was nobody's business. Not only would it put a damper on the reunion, but would make others uncomfortable learning my mom had cheated on my dad. That certainly wasn't a secret Dad would want known. And if the Murrays hadn't yet done their family history and learned I was a genealogist, what if they wanted me to trace their ancestry? Or Dad might be inspired to learn about his Murray line. A line I didn't descend from!

Heat shot up my neck and burst onto my cheeks. My breathing quickened. I inhaled a lungful of air and eased it out, trying to regulate my breathing and extinguish the anger raging inside me. I'd always been closer to my dad than my mom, yet her death had devasted me. Two years later, the sadness over my loss had quickly evolved into anger upon receiving my DNA results. I was still learning to manage that anger, since all it did was raise my blood pressure and take a few days off my life. I closed my eyes, did some yoga breathing, and moved on.

No more energy to chat, I texted Finn, updating him on the case. I promised to give him more details at our dinner. I was looking forward to a night out and cocktails with friends. My mind wandered to what I would wear and what Finn would be wearing...

The ding of an arriving text jarred me. Finn.

That's grand the guards discovered the fella's identity. Looking forward to dinner with the Shovel Slayer.

The nickname had already made it to Finn's dad's pub in Drumcara. I was going to kill Biddy.

I began researching the mysterious Duncan MacDonald from the Isle of Bute. The names Fitzsimmons and Collings weren't listed as a sept—a subdivision—within the Donald (MacDonald) Clan. There were like two hundred sept surnames associated with Scotland's largest clan. Knowing a clan's surnames was helpful since people had often married within a clan. None of the names jumped out at me. For many of them, clan affiliation was dependent on where they hailed from. Pinpointing a *name* was difficult enough.

Not surprisingly, the elderly man had no social media presence. His name also didn't come up in any online church newsletters or social organizations such as the Lion's Club, or articles identifying him as a convicted thief or grave robber.

The statutory register index at ScotlandsPeople had a Duncan MacDonald born in 1929 in the district of Bute. That might be him or not. Original birth records were only available to view on the website after a hundred years. It would likely take four to six weeks to receive a copy via mail. An index on another site noted his mother as Mrs. MacDonald. Big help.

ScotlandsPeople marriage index had a John Duncan MacDonald and Winifred Douglas married in 1949. That was a possibility, even though the surname Douglas also didn't ring any bells. The actual record was only available online seventy-five years after the marriage. At least I was a few *years* shy of it becoming available. Usually, I was merely a few weeks or months away from a needed record's release date, which drove me bananas. Release dates were intended to protect a person's privacy. The 72-Year Rule, a 1978 law, governed the release of the United States Census because seventy-two years was the average life span at the time the law was passed. Every country's policies varied.

My instincts told me Nancy Drew was a woman. If Winifred Douglas was Nancy Drew, maybe she was related one generation further back, so it'd been her mother with a familiar surname. I had to learn her mother's maiden name. Scotland's birth index listed several Winifred Douglases born in Scotland circa the late 1920s, likely the woman's approximate birth year. Who knew if Winifred Douglas was even the mysterious Nancy Drew or if I had the marriage record for the right Duncan MacDonald. And maybe Duncan had promised to bury a sister or cousin with Grandpa, who'd been a relation, making Duncan a relation. Whoever was in the pouch with the necklace must have been somehow related to Grandpa.

The man had registered at Cullen's B & B under a bogus name, so the name he used in Scotland might not have been legit either. Yet he would have had to be awfully savvy or dodgy to forge a passport. I'd see if the minister could provide some insight tomorrow. If Duncan had family in that area at one point, they were likely buried in the church's cemetery. With any luck, in a family plot with headstones going back five generations, including every woman's maiden name.

Family plots had helped me compile several Irish family trees. Before the start of Ireland's civil records in 1864, church records were hit or miss depending on the parish, and they were even scarcer pre-eighteen hundreds. Genealogists relied heavily on gravestone inscriptions. Sadly, families often couldn't afford headstones, especially during the famine, and the wooden crosses were long gone. Sometimes years later a family member erected a memorial to all relations lost during that time period, on occasion including those who'd emigrated. Talk about a gold mine.

I perused online cemetery sites, including Find a Grave and Billion Graves. Around a thousand graves had been transcribed on the Isle of Bute. Not one Fitzsimmons. Fourteen MacDonalds. Not many graves for Scotland's largest clan. The sites relied on volunteers so were far from complete. A local genealogical or historical society might have transcribed the island's cemeteries. Knowing other possible family members buried there was critical.

It would take me days to get to the island by car and ferry and to traipse through all the cemeteries. If I had the time, I'd be all over a road trip to Scotland's graveyards. They were at the top of my cemetery bucket list, along with Paris's. Most people went to Paris to visit the museums displaying impressionist paintings by Degas and Seurat. I couldn't wait to visit the artists' graves.

Eight

AN UNFAMILIAR OFFICER at the Mullingar Garda station handed me my necklace. Thankfully, the tightly fitted clasp had prevented the grainy remains from scratching my grandparents' photos. I tucked my family heirloom safely away into my purse. I'd sanitize it later.

"A decision hasn't yet been made about releasing the remains found on the deceased," the officer said. "My guess is they will likely be returning to Scotland with the body."

"The person needs to be staying here and buried with Mags's grandparents like the fella wanted," Biddy said.

"Is there someone I can talk to about this?" I asked.

I didn't want the remains returned to Scotland until I identified the person. If it was a relative of Grandpa's, it was a relative of mine and should be buried with him, along with Duncan MacDonald. It wouldn't be right to separate the two.

"The sergeant isn't here right now," he said.

Biddy dropped onto the wooden chair next to the officer's desk, which was covered with stacks of files and unfin-ished paperwork. "I'd like to be filing charges."

The officer's gaze narrowed. "Against who?"

"Duncan MacDonald."

"Can't be filing charges against a dead man."

"Is that a law?"

The officer's forehead crinkled. "I'm sure it is. If it's not, it's common sense."

"It's my right to file a charge if I'd like. You can't be sending a criminal back to Scotland. What about the man's fake identity and digging up a grave?"

"The fella's dead." The officer tossed his pen onto the desk. "What more can we be doing to him? And if the post-mortem reveals he died of natural causes, then there's no crime committed *against* him."

A tall red-haired man in tan slacks and a white button-up shirt entered the station.

The officer peered impatiently at us. "Anything else?"

"We're good." I yanked Biddy up from the chair before she could protest.

"I'm Reverend Quinn, here to see Garda Doherty." The red-haired man had an Irish accent, maybe Northern Ireland.

"Garda Doherty isn't out of this station, but I can be helping ya."

Biddy and I exchanged curious looks as we headed toward the door. Was he here to identify Duncan MacDon-ald's body?

"Has to be our man, doesn't he?" Biddy said as soon as we were outside.

I nodded. "Can't be more than thirty. Doubt he'll have

much background on Duncan's family or mine. But it's worth a shot."

Biddy and I waited outside the station for Reverend Quinn. Biddy lay back on the hood of my car, trying to catch a few rays of sunshine, while I blew through antibacterial wipes, cleaning my locket.

The minister exited the building.

I nudged Biddy's leg with my elbow. "We're on."

Biddy slid off the hood, and we headed toward the man.

"Excuse me, Reverend Quinn," I said. "Are you here to identify Duncan MacDonald?"

"Yes, I am." He eyed my blue T-shirt with an amused smile. *Clan Murray. Wreaking Havoc Since the Middle Ages.*

"We're the ones who...discovered his body," I said.

Biddy made the sign of the cross. "If you'd like, we'd be happy to go with you to the mortuary for a bit of moral support."

The man squinted up at the sun in the clear blue sky. "Believe I have all the support I be needing, but thanks a mil for the offer."

"As a nurse, I know how traumatic it can be viewing a dead body. I could be there in case it's too much of a shock for ya."

"I assure you I've seen more than my share of them in my line of work. However, a bit of *financial* support would be welcome. Not sure how the church will manage the high cost of having Duncan MacDonald's body returned to Scotland. The man was a bit of a loner. Will have to take up a special donation. It seems Ireland doesn't provide financial assistance for repatriation, and it's quite dear."

Perfect. The longer it took to raise the funds, the longer I had to figure out both Duncan and Nancy Drew's connection to my grandpa.

Biddy placed a hand on my back. "Mags would be happy to make a donation."

I gave her a tight smile. "As I'm sure Biddy would be also."

A pained expression seized Biddy's face. "Wasn't my grandparents' graves the poor fella died on, but of course I'd be happy to do my part. It's just that working part time, I don't be having a lot of extra cash."

I glared at Biddy, biting my tongue. *Don't you dare play the part-time card when it was your choice!*

"Ah, that's quite kind of you both. Might consider having the cremation done here to help save costs."

"No!" Biddy blurted out, startling the poor guy.

His gaze narrowed. "Against cremation, are ya?"

"I'm against not holding a proper wake for a person, which ya can't be doing if he's cremated." She made the sign of the cross once again. What was up with that?

"The tradition isn't quite as common in Scotland today as it is in Ireland. Besides, wouldn't be holding a wake."

Biddy looked appalled. "Anyone who dies on Irish soil must have a wake."

"A law, is it?" he asked.

"Most certainly is," Biddy lied.

"She's kidding." I shot Biddy a warning glance. She was going to hell for lying to a minister.

Biddy shrugged. "Well, it should be."

"I think money would be better spent on a burial plot," he said.

"He doesn't have a plot?" I said.

There went my idea of checking out the others buried in his family plot or the surrounding area.

"No wake, no burial plot?" Biddy's cheeks reddened. "See, was why the fella came here. To give his loved one a proper burial. Should have gone to bingo last night. Heard Emma Donavan's plot went for almost fifty percent less than what she'd paid. Could have gotten a brill deal for the poor fella and Nancy Drew."

The man's forehead wrinkled in confusion. "Nancy Drew?"

"The remains the man had on him," I said. "Do you know who he might have been burying with my grandparents? Had he a wife who'd recently died?"

"She passed 'bout six years ago."

Biddy made the sign of the cross.

"Was her name Winifred by chance?"

"Frieda, which I suppose could have been a nickname for Winifred."

Hopefully not, since the surname Douglas just added one more unfamiliar name to the mystery.

"Was she cremated?" I asked.

He nodded.

Biddy looked aghast. "So she didn't have a plot either?"

He shook his head.

Biddy opened her mouth for another rant, but I cut her off. "Do you happen to know the woman's maiden name?"

"Not straight off, but I could be checking for you."

"I'd appreciate it. Would like to know if we were somehow related. I believe my grandpa Fitzsimmons, er, maybe Collings, came from Bute. Do you happen to know anyone by either name?"

"Not within the congregation."

"How about Dougal McGuire?" Biddy asked.

His gaze narrowed. "Wasn't he a character on *Father Ted*?"

Biddy snapped her fingers. "Ah, fair play to ya. That's where I'd heard the name before. Father Dougal McGuire. 'Dougal, how did you get into the church? Was it, like, collect twelve crisp packets and become a priest?'" Biddy laughed. "Best line in the entire series."

The minister muffled a laugh, clearly trying not to appear amused by the reference to the irreverent 1990s Irish television comedy.

"Who else would he have been burying besides his wife if he was a loner?" I asked.

The man shrugged.

"Do you think there's anything immoral about acquiring a DNA sample from the man to determine his relationship to Mags?"

The minister's gaze narrowed.

"Nothing intrusive. Merely a few strands of hair or a nail clipping. Could come up with relations to help pay for his return to Scotland and burial costs."

He nodded, taking to the idea. "That it could."

I glared at Biddy before she asked him to obtain fifteen strands of hair from the man.

"What about the man's wife?" I asked. "Had she been a bit more involved with the church?"

"Not particularly."

"I'd greatly appreciate it if you could let me know her death date as well as her maiden name, from either her marriage or death record. If the couple was somehow related to my family, I'd like to contribute to the burial."

The minister smiled. "Most certainly will. Should be able to get back to you within a few days."

I scrawled my email on a sticky note from my purse, and he slipped it into his pants pocket. "Let us know if there is anything else we can do to help."

"Like help clean out the fella's place," Biddy said.

"The ladies' church group is boxing up his belongings but doubt they'll make much selling 'em. He lived a simple life."

"No!" Biddy and I blurted out, causing the man to flinch.

"We mean, we'd like to assist them, if needed," I said.

"No worries. They're almost finished."

No belongings, no cemetery plot, no friends, and no wake. No need for a road trip to the Isle of Bute. We couldn't find clues in an empty house. And it was beyond sad that the man's entire life could be tossed into a few boxes and sold to strangers at a thrift shop. The thought of them packing up old family photos, or worse yet, throwing them out, made my heart ache. What if Duncan MacDonald's belongings included photos?

"Would you mind asking the ladies to put aside any photos they come across? I'll pay to have them shipped. I'd really like them should I discover I'm related to the man."

If it turned out that I wasn't related to him, I'd still end up keeping the pictures. I wouldn't be able to bring myself to part with old family photos even if the people in them weren't my family.

"Did he ever happen to go to confession?" Biddy asked.

"The Presbyterian faith doesn't require a person to discuss his weaknesses and sins with his minister to receive forgiveness from God. Even if he'd confided in me, I couldn't divulge that."

Biddy's gaze narrowed. "So are ya saying he did tell ya something?" She slipped a bill from her wallet. "I'd be happy to be making a twenty-euro donation right now."

He snatched the bill from Biddy's hand. "That's quite kind of you. Now, I must be going." He headed off for the mortuary.

I smacked Biddy's arm. "Can't believe you just tried to bribe a minister. Have you no shame? Even worse, what if he doesn't forward me the information he'd promised?"

"Wasn't bribing him. Merely offering a donation."

"Thought you couldn't be making a donation now that you work *part time*?"

She shrugged. "Would be much cheaper for you to hold the wake here and have him buried in Ireland."

"I'm not paying to have him or Nancy Drew buried anywhere until I know if we're related. I'm not spending eternity next to some strangers."

If I decided to bury them in my family plot, Reverend Quinn would likely hand over the remains quite willingly if it meant not having to fund the repartition.

Nine

CULLEN'S B & B was an impressive Georgian-style stone house located down a narrow rural road about ten miles from my home. Three dormer windows lined the roof, with a brick chimney on each end. White lace curtains hung in the upstairs guest-room windows, while open green drapes on the lower level provided a view of a sitting room.

"Hopefully, she has a clue about that Duncan fella," Biddy said as we headed up the cobblestone walk lined with colorful flowers. "Maybe he'd mentioned Scotland or why he was visiting the area."

"I doubt the man would have confided in a stranger that he was here to dig up a grave and add remains."

"If he was a loner, he might have been needing someone to talk to. He certainly couldn't have confided in his judgmental minister."

"Gee, a minister who's judgmental about some woman trying to bribe him. Imagine that."

Biddy jutted out her chin. "Guess he's not the only judgmental one."

I rang the doorbell next to the green wooden door. A woman in her eighties with short gray hair, dressed in casual tan slacks and a white blouse, answered with a smile. We exchanged introductions with the owner, Breeda Cullen.

Her blue eyes widened. "Mags Murray? The woman who found the fella in the cemetery robbing her grandparents' graves?"

I nodded. "He wasn't actually robbing the graves. More like donating to them."

Her eyes lit with excitement, and she ushered us inside. "Well, how were you supposed to know that? You had every right to defend yourself."

I gave her a tight smile. "I didn't hit him over the head with a shovel. He was dead when I found him."

She tilted her head, as if sizing me up, trying to determine if I looked capable of killing the man.

"Don't think I'd be here now if that were the case. I'd be in jail."

"Suppose not. I told Madeline that didn't sound right you being let off because the jails are too full and too few guards to be making your arrest yet."

"I'd appreciate it if you could set people straight."

She nodded, yet the glint in her eyes was far from reassuring. She led us into the sitting room, where guests could enjoy complimentary cookies and tea. The cream-colored room with emerald-green furniture and drapes was currently empty. Biddy and I sat on a velvet couch.

Breeda poured tea and placed a plate of chocolate-covered biscuits on a white cocktail table. Almost dinnertime, my stomach growled and I reached for a cookie.

The woman shook her head. "This whole thing is causing

quite the unrest. Now that people are selling off plots in Ballycaffey, St. Mary's up the road is raising prices, taking advantage of the situation. Father Davies should be ashamed of himself. Parishioners will likely demand he be sent back to England before long. Thankfully, Andrew and I have had our plots for years."

I was becoming more appreciative of the burial plots I'd inherited. Otherwise, Biddy might have been burying me with my grandparents. Who knew how many people would end up in my family plot?

A middle-aged couple back from a day of touring shrugged off their lightweight jackets while heading straight for the tea and cookies station.

"Did you get to know Duncan MacDonald while he was staying here?" I asked Breeda.

"I must confess, I avoided having a conversation with the man if at all possible. His Scottish brogue was more than a wee bit difficult to understand. He didn't seem receptive to chatting anyway."

"Sorry. Not to be eavesdropping about that Scottish fella," the woman tourist said, filling her teacup. "But don't think he could have been all bad, having that lovely floral wreath for decorating the grave."

Even tourists had heard the story? And what wreath?

"Ah, that's right," her husband said. "Irish writing on the ribbon, there was. It's grand seeing people still using the language."

"At least the fella felt a bit of remorse for digging up that grave," the woman said. "Quite a lovely wreath, wasn't it?" She peered over at Breeda.

Breeda nodded faintly. "Yes, quite lovely indeed."

Biddy and I exchanged curious glances. Had we been too traumatized by the dead body to notice a lovely wreath?

"What did it look like?" I asked the couple.

"Was yellow and green with a white ribbon," the woman said.

The two guests left, and we returned to our conversation with Breeda.

"Was the man by chance a smoker?" Biddy asked. "Maybe threw his butts out on the walk?"

Breeda shook her head. "Not that I recall."

"Any other bad habits, like flossing his teeth at the breakfast table or sticking chewing gum on a plate?"

She shook her head.

"Could we perhaps see his room?" I asked, rescuing the poor woman from Biddy's interrogation on possible DNA samples.

"I suppose. Don't see why not. Gardai collected all the man's belongings. The woman who cleans isn't due until tomorrow. Not sure she'll be up to cleaning it if she heard the man died, even if it wasn't in the room. A bit superstitious, she is."

Breeda showed us to a room with light-green walls and white furnishings. A rose-colored duvet lay in a pile at the end of the double bed, and the empty armoire doors were open. The room might be dirty, but it had been cleaned out except for a few tissues in the small garbage can. We slipped on a pair of latex gloves and began our search.

Biddy tied the top of the plastic garbage bag and stuffed it in her large purse. "You said DNA testing is evolving rapidly, and next week or month we might be able to test these."

She checked under the bed and mattress while I removed

each dresser drawer to make sure nothing had been taped to the bottom or behind that the guards might have missed. It wasn't like the room was a crime scene, or they'd been searching for evidence to build a case against the guy.

Biddy rubbed a pencil lightly across the top sheet of paper on a notepad to see what was written on the previous sheet. "Collect at Jimmy's seven p.m. Wonder who Jimmy is?"

"I think he means Jimmy's takeaway place up the road."

Before leaving, we thanked Breeda for her hospitality. She sent us on our way with to-go cups of tea and ginger biscuits.

"How rude, digging up a grave without even leaving flowers," Biddy said as we walked to the car. "We needn't be so worried about proper DNA etiquette when he wasn't concerned about proper burial etiquette."

"If the flowers weren't for my grandparents' graves, then whose grave did he put them on?"

"Think the guards or Marjorie Walsh's gossip minions would have mentioned another dug-up grave."

I called Garda Doherty and inquired about whether a wreath had been found in the man's room or his car. One hadn't been. The officer wasn't even curious enough to ask why I was inquiring about the wreath.

Whose grave had Duncan MacDonald put the lovely wreath on?

We stopped at the Ballycaffey cemetery to see if a wreath resembling Duncan MacDonald's had been placed on a neighboring grave while the man was digging up my grandma's. It wasn't there. It also wasn't on Lucy Fitzsimmons Cavanaugh's grave. Except for a shared surname, I hadn't linked the woman to Grandpa despite numerous attempts, including locating her obituary a few months ago. I'd finally come to the conclusion there likely wasn't a connection, and I had to let it go. Clues often took you down a wrong path for hours or even months. As the joke went, *Only a genealogist views a step backward as progress*. Once you ruled out a clue, you could move onto the next one, which might take you down the right path. Besides a sense of humor, a successful genealogist needed perseverance and an optimistic outlook. My sense of humor and optimism were quickly fading. Good thing I had the perseverance of a squirrel trying to raid a squirrel-proof bird feeder.

We did a quick sweep of the cemetery, finding numerous decorated graves, but no yellow-and-green wreath with Irish writing on a white ribbon. We walked out the main gate and encountered Gretta clipping the grass along the outside of the stone wall. It appeared she'd been granted the caretaker position as part of her community service hours.

"Janey Mac," Biddy muttered, eyeing Gretta's pitch-black hair. "Looks like she just rose from a grave herself. Forget a grave gun or coffin torpedo. The mere sight of the woman would be scaring away any body snatchers."

The contrast of Gretta's black hair against her pale skin was a bit creepy. You'd think with all her time outside on rubbish patrol, she'd have gotten a bit of color on her skin. It had been an unusually dry and sunny summer.

"My mum could likely correct your color, at least a bit," Biddy told Gretta.

The woman gave Biddy a tight smile. "This was the color

I was hoping for, except a wee bit more auburn would have been grand. It's a lovely change after having the white for so many years."

Biddy nodded. "Ah, that's grand, isn't it now?" She peered over at me, still nodding with an overly enthusiastic smile.

I nodded in agreement.

Gretta stood, brushing the dirt from the knees of her tan cotton pants. "Been keeping an eye on the place the past few days. Appears that man's attempt at digging up your grand-parents' graves was a one-off. Not much going on here except it seems to be a popular spot for a bit of how's your father with the young ones."

How romantic. Making out in a cemetery with your boyfriend.

"Emma Donovan was here showing off her plot to the new owner. Been wanting an excuse for years to not be buried next to her husband. Her seizing the opportunity has caused a selling spree of plots. Woman should be ashamed. If the cemetery shuts down, she'll be to blame."

I described the wreath to Gretta in case it had been here but was now gone.

She shook her head. "Think I'd remember having seen a wreath with Irish writing. Not so common nowadays. And I've walked the entire cemetery a dozen times. Should ya be needing assistance in locating it, I'd be happy to help."

"We're grand, thanks," Biddy said.

"Actually, that'd be great if you could check out some other cemeteries for the wreath."

Biddy glared at me.

Gretta's determined gaze peered into the distance. "If that wreath is out there, I'll be finding it."

"See Edmond Collier for a list of cemeteries within a twenty-mile radius, including abandoned ones in the middle of sheep fields. Better take aluminum foil. If the wreath is on a stone too weathered to read, molding the foil against it will help with transcribing."

Gretta nodded. "I'll be on it first thing tomorrow." She went back to trimming grass.

"What are ya doing asking that woman for help?" Biddy said as we headed toward the car.

"I didn't ask her—she offered."

"Whatever. The witch gave me the creeps even before she looked like the walking dead."

"The woman hit you in the side of the head with a mushy tomato. She whacked me over the head with her lead purse that landed me in the ER. I let it go. You need to get over it."

"A mushy tomato that ruined my makeup and hairdo and my one shot at scoring a date with that young Sean Connery look-alike fella at the *Rags to Riches Roadshow* filming."

"Get over it. Would you rather search cemeteries for the wreath or help me question Kiernan Moffat?"

"Fine."

That wouldn't have been my answer. If I had a choice, I'd rather pack a picnic lunch and spend a sunny day wandering through cemeteries than spending fifteen minutes questioning the dodgy appraiser.

We entered McCarthy's pub needing a pint before individually bagging a dead man's tissues. The two men from the night before were there again playing darts.

The one in a red sports jersey raised his pint. "To the Defender of the Dead."

"The Tombstone Terminator," his John Deere buddy said.

The other man smiled. "Ah, that's grand. Tombstone Terminator. Was a lovely movie, it was, with Arnold Schwarzenegger." They clinked glasses and polished off their pints.

I wouldn't call the movie *The Terminator*, or my nickname, lovely.

A younger guy holding a pool stick poked his head out from the adjoining room. "Conan, Keeper of the Crypt."

The men raised their empty glasses in approval.

"I appreciate your support," I told them. "But if the guards catch wind of my nicknames, they might get the wrong idea."

Their brows crinkled with confusion.

"That I'm guilty of killing the man when I'm not."

"Ah, right, then." The John Deere guy nodded, looking skeptical.

Biddy's dad had a cider and salt 'n' vinegar potato chips waiting for me on the bar. "Kind of like that Tombstone Terminator one." He grinned.

"Don't humor them." I smiled thanks and took several gulps of cider.

"Ah, grand. Auntie Violet dropped off the urn." Biddy nodded at a bronze statue of a cow next to the register behind the bar.

Daniel eyed the cow. "An urn, is it? Thought it was a statue."

"Don't feel bad. Uncle Seamus thought it was a doorstop."

He held up a halting hand. "Don't even want to be knowing why you need an urn. Or why you're carrying a bag of garbage and latex gloves. Your mum filled me in on what you two have been up to. Just don't be getting into trouble tampering with a corpse."

"If Mags becomes the caretaker of Nancy Drew, the remains need a proper storage place besides a velvet pouch."

He shook his head and walked over to serve patrons.

"Before we go through the garbage, we need to be taking care of your locket. I have everything set for the smudging ceremony to rid the necklace of the negative energy from being stored with the remains."

Three months ago our search for Aidan Neil and the family's manuscript had led us to the famous author Brendan Quigley's house in Cork, to question Valerie Burke, the author's estate manager. Biddy was convinced the house was haunted by the author's sinister mind. She'd brought along the only sage in her house, an herb jar of crushed sage leaves. After that she'd stocked up on sage bundles and all the accessories for conducting a smudging ritual.

"You're okay with me burying a possible stranger's remains with my grandparents, yet it's too traumatic for my *locket* to have been in a pouch with them?"

"Burning sage releases negative ions, which is known for putting people in a more positive mood." She gave me a pointed look. "It can clear up ninety percent of airborne bacteria, unlike your wipes."

Fine. I followed Biddy behind the bar toward the door into their residence.

"Take that thing with you." Biddy's dad gestured to the urn.

I grabbed the urn, hoping it was empty. If it turned out I was related to Nancy Drew, I certainly wouldn't be storing the person in a secondhand urn. It could use a good smudging itself. What type of person sold a used urn?

After a one-hour smudging ceremony and two cider ales, I went home smelling like burning grass. A faint pungent smell, like the grass you smoke. I placed the cow urn in the mudroom. Biddy had insisted I take it home even though there was no way I was putting anyone's remains in a used urn, related or not. And the idea of the urn possibly being occupied at the moment gave me the creeps.

I barely had the strength to shove the coatrack in front of the door. Besides going on little sleep, paranoia was quite draining. I didn't have the brainpower for a night of mental gymnastics conducting genealogy research. I needed to be well rested and on my game when visiting Kiernan Moffat. However, I did a quick check of my DNA accounts for MacDonald or Douglas matches. Dozens of MacDonald matches came up. No surprise. It was one of the top ten most common surnames in Scotland. However, it barely made the top one hundred most common Irish surnames. Only a handful of matches had trees, and no two contained a common ancestor.

I had a handful of Douglas matches. Douglas barely

squeaked into the top hundred most common Scottish surnames and didn't make the list in Ireland. The closest match shared second or third great-grandparents. That might have been a close enough match to pique my curiosity if I'd known my biological father's sixteen second great-grandparents' surnames or thirty-two third great-grandparents'.

I set the security system, threw on my pj's, popped two sleeping pills, and pushed the dresser in front of my bedroom door. I collapsed onto the bed, hoping that visions of Duncan MacDonald's eerie, gray-eyed gaze wouldn't keep me awake all night. I closed my eyes, and Kiernan Moffat's blue eyes stared back at me from behind a pair of wire glasses, and the scent of spearmint gum filled my head. My eyes shot open. The forty-five-year-old appraiser's average good looks weren't nearly as haunting as the dead man's, but the thought of once again seeing the shady character was a bit unnerving.

Yet something told me that Kiernan Moffat had a clue as to the reason behind the theft of my family heirloom.

Ten

Rags to Riches Roadshow was filming at Russborough House, located in northern Wicklow, near the Wicklow Mountains. The stately home had quite the colorful past. The estate had been the site of four art thefts, three extended families, two forced occupations by the British and IRA during civil wars, and one ghost—who'd experienced it all since the house was built in 1755. Usually, the ghost stories would have intrigued me the most. However, I found it interesting that Kiernan Moffat was filming at an estate with a history of stolen works of priceless art, like Vermeer and Goya. Maybe the appraiser had chosen the filming site to case the joint. If art theft number five occurred in the near future, I wouldn't be surprised.

Yet would I share my suspicions with the authorities? Kiernan Moffat might have been locked up three months ago had I pursued the appraiser's involvement in the Neil case. A good thing I hadn't gone after him, since I now needed his help. How crazy was that? I had to keep this man out of prison in case I needed to rely on his expertise once again.

However, I certainly wasn't the only person who suspected the appraiser wasn't on the up and up. Albert had his suspicions too.

Biddy and I walked down the gravel drive toward the massive stone house, which boasted the longest facade in Ireland. The main building was flanked by open-air walks lined with columns and nooks showcasing statues. At the end of each walk stood a smaller building. When we reached the steps leading to the home's main entrance, I finished polishing my locket and the small gold key with a soft cloth and clasped it around my neck. Wearing the necklace after it had been with the remains made the hairs on my neck prickle.

"You keep buffing that yoke and you're gonna wear off the floral engraving," Biddy said. "It's grand. The sage cleansing did the trick."

The woman who'd been responsible for determining the lottery winners, and selecting Biddy's butt-ugly painting, wasn't there today. However, it was the same security guard. A middle-aged man who loved the ladies. A bit of flirting and lying, claiming that Kiernan Moffat had invited us, gained us access to the film site.

We found the man in the library, an appropriate location for appraising vintage books. The room's green wallpaper was a darker shade where artwork had once hung. After the thefts, some paintings were never recovered, while others had been donated to museums for safekeeping. An ornate antique desk and more modern red furniture sat on a blue-and-green worn rug covering the wood floor.

Kiernan Moffat spotted us approaching. He inhaled a surprised gasp along with his spearmint gum. He let out a series of coughs, pounding a fist against his chest and a green tie that matched the darker shade of wallpaper. His eyes watering behind the wire glasses, he plucked a white handkerchief from the breast pocket of his navy blazer and got his coughing fit under control. The locket around my neck put a twinkle back in his blue eyes.

I filled him in on the theft and wanting to have my heirloom appraised in case it was stolen again. I also wanted to gauge his reaction to the thief, just to satisfy my curiosity. "The man's name was Duncan MacDonald or possibly Dougal McGuire, from Scotland."

Rather than nervous gum chewing or a suspicious glint in his eyes, the appraiser laughed. "Serious, are ya? Dougal McGuire was a character on *Father Ted*. A brilliant one at that."

Biddy shook her head. "Still can't believe that name didn't click with me straight away."

Biddy prided herself on being able to name almost every character on popular TV shows, including those before she was even born, such as *Coronation Street*, which first aired in 1960.

From the appraiser's reaction, I was further convinced the man hadn't conspired with Duncan MacDonald to steal my locket.

"Outside of watches, jewelry isn't my specialty." He admired the vintage Rolex on his wrist. His annoying habit of constantly checking the time was to draw attention to his expensive watches, not because he had so many places to go and important people to see. He glanced up from his watch to my locket, the tip of the gold heart just shy of touching the neckline of my white blouse. "If I were to hazard a guess, I'd say it's of the Victorian era. No precious stones would certainly decrease its value. I would estimate two thousand euros."

As if a piece worth a *mere* twenty-five hundred dollars would have caught his eye. I'd always wondered if part of his scam was to appraise an item on the low end so a partner could swoop in and buy it for cheap, then turn around and sell it for beaucoup bucks.

I quirked a brow. "You're sure that's all?"

He shrugged. "Like I told the woman a few years back with an identical piece, the value—"

"Wait, what? A woman had an identical necklace to mine?" Goose bumps skittered across my skin.

He nodded. "As I was saying, that wasn't what intrigued me. It was the contents of her locket. Most certainly Victorian mourning jewelry."

"Like on *Downton Abbey*, where they changed outfits for every meal, they also changed jewelry?" Biddy asked.

The appraiser scoffed. "*Mourning*, as in bereaved. When someone died, he or she would bequeath a piece of jewelry to each heir as a memento. Those who could afford to do so would often have a quantity of items made up to distribute to close family and friends at the memorial service."

"This locket was passed down in my grandpa's family. You think it was a piece of mourning jewelry?" My heart tapped faster than an Irish step dancer.

"Quite likely. It has the same key charm as the other woman's, which was what caught my eye. Pieces were customized for the deceased with a charm, family crest, the person's name or initials, among other things."

"Like a floral design if the person was a gardener?" I gestured to the engraving on the front of my locket.

"Precisely. That woman's piece also had a similar design and the same sturdy Belcher chain with the thick rounded links. The jewelry was common among the well-to-do, especially in the Victorian era. When Prince Albert died, Queen Victoria took bereavement to a whole new level, wearing black the remaining forty years of her life and a mourning locket with a photo of her late husband. Lockets became quite en vogue in the early 1860s. You'd be best off speaking to my friend, who collects mourning jewelry. He'd be better able to pinpoint a date and give you more insight."

"Eeewww." Biddy's top lip curled back. "Who would collect such a morbid thing?"

He gave Biddy a mental eye roll and turned to me. "May I see the inside of your locket?"

I clicked open the clasp and revealed my grandparents' photos.

He let out a disappointed sigh. "The snap in that woman's locket was of a lady quite alluring for her age and having been dead. With an elaborate hairstyle and dress that made me believe she was from an affluent family."

"She was *dead* in the photo?" I clutched my locket, which had likely once contained the picture of a dead ancestor.

He nodded. "But her dog was quite alive. An English springer spaniel, if I recall correctly." He smiled. "Cute lad. Would have named him Archie if he'd been mine."

Ireland's dog license registrations for the eighteen hundreds and early nineteen hundreds were available online. I doubted the index was searchable according to breeds.

"Collecting photos of dead people you're not even related to? How mad is that?" The color drained from Biddy's face.

I was prepared to fan her with an antique book from the occasional table next to me.

"Postmortem photography was popular in the Victorian era. Would have been no different than taking a wedding snap."

"Except you're *alive* at your wedding," Biddy said.

"Some surely wish they were dead." He smirked at Biddy. "Having the original snap in the locket would make it all the more enticing for a collector. And the other side of that woman's piece held a woven lock of the deceased's hair, making it even more valuable."

"Too bad mine didn't still have the lock of hair since we might soon be able to have the DNA tested," I said.

"My grandma kept a snippet of hair from my mum's and her sister's first haircuts. It was believed to bring good luck." Biddy winced. "Couldn't imagine her having cut another lock if one of them had died."

Yet Biddy was fine yanking hair from a dead stranger's head.

"Anything distinguishing about the photo?" I asked. "Like the photographer's studio name embossed in the corner?"

"Don't recall. Was likely a bit small of a snap for that."

"When was the other woman on the show?" I asked.

"She didn't appear on the episode. Was beat out by a stuffed rabbit thought to have once been part of King George the Fifth's collection. Her information should be on file. We keep track of every appraisal regardless of whether the person is on the show. I can check into that for you. I referred her to my collector friend Edgar Bates for more information and a more accurate appraisal. Feel free to call in on him at his Dublin shop. See if she was ever in touch. He'd be better able to give insight into your necklace."

"Where had you been filming that episode?"

"Belfast."

The city my grandpa had often visited. Interesting.

So she'd likely lived in the city or nearby since the show filmed all over Ireland and the UK. Or had she taken a ferry over from the Isle of Bute, Scotland?

"Did she have a Scottish accent?" I asked.

"Not that I recall, but that was a few years ago."

"Do you remember anything else about her?"

"She was a bit older than yourself, with dark hair...or maybe it was blond..."

He could remember the breed of the dog in the photo yet had no recollection what the *living* locket owner had looked like.

"Was it common to bury the piece of jewelry with a family member?" Biddy asked.

The appraiser's top lip curled back. As if burying the jewelry would be worse than collecting it. "I would think not. The idea was to wear it in memory of the deceased. Would seem a bit irreverent to bury it, I'd say. Unless, of course, one hadn't much cared for the person, I suppose. If we can locate the other woman, this would make quite a fascinating episode and might help you locate others with the same locket. Sadly, the show doesn't resume filming until September."

"I certainly hope I've solved the mystery by then."

Biddy perked up, the color returning to her cheeks. "Starring in another episode would be grand."

Starring? More like *appearing* in an episode, wasn't it?

"The solved mystery might make an even more intriguing story," he said. "How you came to locate relations with the same jewelry piece." He framed the air with his hands. "Mourning jewelry. Commemorating the dead and uniting the living."

The appraiser gave me his friend's contact information. He also promised to seek out details on the woman with the locket. Quite possibly my relation. Good thing I hadn't had the man investigated.

Biddy shuddered as we walked out the front door and down the stone steps. "Forget what I said. Keep buffing away on your locket, and we'll do another sage cleansing when we get home. That's mad that your locket once held a dead woman's hair and photo."

"Having a photo and lock of hair from an ancestor isn't nearly as creepy as collecting hundreds of strangers' hair and funeral photos."

Biddy nodded. "Will definitely need to be stocking up on sage before calling in on his collector friend. Just his name, Edgar Bates, makes my skin crawl. No time to be ordering sage online." She Googled area shops selling sage bundles. "There's a candle shop twenty minutes north on our way home."

I suddenly remembered that we were going out for dinner.

"It has to be a quick stop. I have a ton to do before we meet Finn and Collin for dinner tonight." No time to wash my hair—I'd have to throw it up in a clip. Thankfully, I'd bought a new dress, so that saved a half hour trying to decide what to wear. "If I can find that woman with the other locket, maybe she'll take a DNA test. Or maybe she's already a match of mine. If mourning jewelry was customized for the deceased, what's the chance she's not related to my grandpa? Maybe she knows our family history." My mind raced with possibilities!

"Unless her granny collected mourning jewelry."

"He said she was confident it was her ancestor in the photo."

"Would you be telling the truth if your granny collected dead people's hair and photos rather than teacups?"

"If Nancy Drew was my grandpa's sister, she would have had her own necklace if it'd been memorializing his mother or father. Unless she'd lost hers. Maybe the necklace goes back more generations, so there'd only been one to pass down."

"Take a snap of yourself wearing the locket and holding a sign that you're searching for long-lost rellies. Posts like that always go viral."

"Duncan MacDonald might have seen me wearing the locket on TV and recognized the family heirloom. He figured out where I lived, then stole it and tried to bury it with the remains. Who knows what weirdos social media might attract? That was a last resort. I'll start by contacting Simon Reese and our shared DNA matches to see if anyone recognizes the necklace. Only one responded to my message a few months ago. I'll bet they'll be more intrigued by this discovery and apt to respond. I'll entice them with the possibility of appearing on an episode of *Rags to Riches Roadshow*."

"Oh yeah, contacting DNA matches worked out well for Aidan Neil, getting him kidnapped, shot, and almost killed."

"As if my necklace is worth anywhere near an alleged Brendan Quigley manuscript."

I opened the locket and focused on Grandpa's photo, trying to send a psychic message out into the universe. *What is the key to your mysterious past? And whose photo did yours replace?* The locket possibly having been a family heirloom is likely what my grandma meant by it being the *key* to more than Grandpa's heart. She meant it unlocked the treasure trove of family history.

Now that I knew there were possibly other lockets out there besides that one woman's, I had to find them!

On the way to the sage shop, I called Garda Doherty, who confirmed that the autopsy had ruled out foul play. Duncan MacDonald had died of a heart attack. I almost collapsed with relief. No more triple-checking my security system or having to shove furniture in front of the doors before going to bed. That better put an end to the Shovel Slayer and Tombstone Terminator rumors. Actually, it was nice to know the locals had my back should I ever be accused of murder.

"If he died of a heart attack, maybe that's why he chose now to bury Nancy Drew's remains," Biddy said. "He knew he didn't have long to live."

I nodded. "We'll never know. The case is officially closed. The downside is his body can now be sent back to Scotland early next week if Reverend Quinn comes up with the funds.

I need to determine Nancy Drew's identity ASAP. Once Duncan's and Nancy's remains are off to Scotland, I'll have to get permission to dig them up. Yet without a burial plot, the two of them will likely be spread over the Isle of Bute or in the Irish Sea, and there'd be nothing to exhume."

Right now the bodies were in limbo.

Thankfully, I no longer was, now that I knew I was looking for family members with the same locket. I just had to find them. Hopefully Edgar Bates could help confirm my connection to the Belfast woman. A creepy feeling slithered over me as I imagined Kiernan Moffat's collector friend sheathed in black, a mourning ring on each of his bony yellow-nail fingers.

Eleven

⌒⌒⌒

WE ARRIVED home an hour later than planned, thanks to Biddy getting lost on the way to the candle shop. She'd bought the store out of sage bundles. It'd taken her a half hour to decide which sage scent smelled best: juniper, lavender, citrus... By the time we left the shop, I was feeling far from Zen or *cleansed*, reeking like I'd just spent the afternoon walking through perfume counters at a department store. I had research to conduct and dinner with Finn in two hours. No time for another smudging ceremony, Biddy doused me in lavender sage spray before I could escape her car.

I pulled a stack of old family photo albums from my office shelf and plopped down in the chair at Grandma's desk. I paged through them, searching for a locket-size picture of a dead woman. Maybe I'd previously come across the photo and had assumed the woman was merely resting peacefully. I'd never have expected to find a photo of a dead ancestor in our family albums. However, Grandma had once mentioned having several photos of ancestors' wakes. Had she meant photos of the *deceased* rather than guests celebrating the person's life? If such photos existed, Grandma had likely kept them out of the albums not wanting to traumatize her young granddaughter who'd spend hours looking through them.

Many of the photos had people's names written in ink across their outfits or foreheads. Others had faded names scrawled in pencil on the back. Maybe the pictures without names were Grandpa's relations. Unless I found the locket photo and compared it to ones from when the woman was alive, I wouldn't be able to confirm a connection.

I continued perusing the albums until I came up empty. No tiny photo of a dead woman. If I found the photo, I could upload it to Google Images and maybe have better luck than I'd had with Duncan MacDonald's photo. A DNA forum member had once done an online search of a vintage wedding photo. The same photo had appeared on a family historian's personal website with the family tree traced back three centuries. I'd be happy to hook up with someone whose tree went back three *generations*. The search engine seemed to do better when focusing on one detail in the photo...

Like a locket!

I anxiously loaded the photo of my locket, hoping it'd show up on an antique shop's website or some lady's neck on her LinkedIn profile picture. Many similar ones popped up: gold, heart-shaped, fancy engraving on the front... But none that were identical to mine, with a key on a gold chain. Good to know that hundreds of the same locket weren't being auctioned off on eBay for twenty bucks. Further evidence that my necklace had been a customized piece of mourning jewelry.

My phone rang. Edmond. I'd gotten his voice mail earlier

when I'd called to tell him about my mourning jewelry discovery. He asked me to stop over, so I hopped into my car to pay him a quick visit, only having an hour and fifteen minutes until dinner.

When I arrived at Edmond's, he and Rosie were washing dishes in the pale-yellow kitchen. The scent of Rosie's specialty lamb covered in a secret brown sauce filled the air. My stomach lurched.

"Oh, you just missed dinner," Rosie said. "But I'd be happy to heat you up a plate. Would only take but a moment." She opened the refrigerator door, preparing to remove the leftovers.

Rather than the usual lonely takeaway container or two and a carton of eggs, the fridge now held plastic containers with leftovers, fresh produce, and a variety of juices. White curtains hung on the once-bare kitchen windows. A spice rack and a variety of jams had joined a whiskey bottle on the white countertop. Edmond's bachelor pad had been in desperate need of Rosie's caring touch.

I smiled. "Thanks, but I'm meeting friends for dinner."

Even if I hadn't had dinner plans, I'd have lied. Rosie had served the dish once when Biddy and I had paid her a visit. I'd managed to discreetly slip Biddy my portion, not wanting to offend the woman by getting sick on her fine china.

We went into the living room for tea. It was going to be a long night, and I needed to offset the lavender sage spray, so I didn't hesitate to consume caffeine. I sat in the rocking chair next to them on the couch and recounted my visit with Kiernan Moffat and his lesson on mourning jewelry.

"What an exciting discovery," Rosie said. "And my

brother Albert sent the photo of your locket to dozens of fellow antique shop owners and had a hit."

I stopped rocking in the chair. "He did?"

"A shop owner in Edinburgh bought one a few years back. As he recalled, the woman who sold it was moving to Australia."

"I don't care how desperate I was—I'd never sell a family heirloom."

"She mightn't have known it was an heirloom," Edmond said. "You hadn't known the entire story behind yours."

I still didn't.

"Now that I think of it, my friend Mary once had a brooch with a lovely work of art weaved from hair," Rosie mused. "It most certainly had been a piece of mourning jewelry. I'll have Albert ask the shop owner if he recalls the locket containing the deceased's snap or lock of hair. The man offered to look back through his paperwork to see if he can find the buyer's name and a photo of the locket."

"That'd be wonderful, thanks," I said. "It's worth a shot. The woman with the locket at the Roadshow filming was from the Belfast area. Funny how that city is suddenly popping up everywhere."

Edmond quirked a brow. "Most certainly is, isn't it?"

"I can't imagine that we're not somehow related. Might help me determine the person in the pouch's connection to my grandpa. Duncan MacDonald's death was ruled a heart attack, so his body will return to Scotland next week, along with the remains in the pouch. I feel if they are my family, they should be buried with my grandparents, like Duncan wanted. Don't you think?"

"I think that's your decision, luv," Edmond said. "But Maggie would have approved."

"Would there be a wake?" Rosie asked.

I shrugged. "Not sure. Likely not, since he didn't know anyone from the area."

"Well, if there is, I'd like the opportunity to sew the button on the fella's jacket and hem his slacks. The man should have a proper suit for his wake."

That was a lot of trouble to go to when he'd be cremated. Not wishing to seem unappreciative or to upset Rosie, I smiled. "That'd be nice."

Walking from Biddy's car to the restaurant, I tucked a few stray strands of hair back up in the clip, applied pink lipstick, and double-checked that I'd penciled in my missing sliver of eyebrow. After getting home from Edmond's, I'd barely had time to swap out my T-shirt and jeans for my new blue sundress, only to discover a tear in the seam. I'd had to go with a pair of new jeans, a white lace blouse, and sandals. I'd thrown myself together on the fifteen-minute bumpy ride to Castleroche, having to correct my eyebrow several times after hitting a pothole.

Whereas Biddy had apparently started preparing for a night out the second she'd gotten home after dropping me off. Her dark-blond hair was free of its usual ponytail, curls bouncing in rhythm with her steps. She'd gone all out with eyeliner and shadow, which she'd constantly checked in the rearview mirror on the way there. She wore a formfitting green dress and tan wedge heels.

She was awfully spiffed up for this *not* being a date.

I knew Biddy and Collin saw each other more often than she admitted. I hadn't seen Finn or Collin since the Jerry Springer DNA meeting last month when they'd helped me tear apart the brawling couple. Finn had suggested Oscar's restaurant rather than his dad's pub. Perfect. Nobody at the restaurant would likely know me as the Tombstone Terminator or Shovel Slayer. However, the restaurant's quaint exterior definitely had more of a date feel. Ivy trailed from the window boxes and across the stone facade. Iron lanterns lit each side of the wood door we approached.

I grabbed Biddy's arm, bringing her to a halt. "Don't kiss Collin hello."

"Ah, okay."

"Or hug."

"Should we be shaking hands?"

"Just don't touch at all. That'd make it awkward for Finn and me."

"Do you ever plan on kissing Finn?"

I shrugged. "Yeah, sometime, I'm sure. Just don't want to be smearing my freshly applied lipstick."

"Then why are you here?" Biddy opened the door and breezed inside without waiting for an answer, which I didn't have.

The restaurant's ambiance reminded me of a French wine cellar. Stone walls, rustic wood tables with flickering candles, and iron chairs with fancy scrollwork backs and thick red cushions on the seats. Finn and Collin gave us a wave from a table next to an unlit fireplace. They pushed back their chairs and stood to greet us. Finn was several inches taller than Collin, with darker brown hair. Both had blue eyes, but Finn's thick dark lashes made his eyes look even bluer.

Collin gave me a sympathetic smile and a quick hug. So much for no touching. "How ya doing? Can't believe ya found a dead fella on your grandparents' graves. But that's grand the postmortem proved you're not the Shovel Slayer."

"Did it now?" Finn said.

Biddy's glare wiped the smile from Collin's face.

"Oh, sorry. Shouldn't be mentioning Shovel Slayer. If it makes you feel better, Biddy didn't tell me the nickname. Heard it from the lads at the pub."

No, that didn't make me feel better.

And that wasn't the reason for Biddy's glare. We'd just learned the autopsy results a few hours ago. Biddy had obviously talked to Collin despite the fact we were meeting for dinner. They spoke more frequently than she admitted. More frequently than Finn and me. Finn had just learned about the autopsy results from Collin.

The no-touching rule was out the window, so Biddy and Collin hugged hello. Finn came around the table for our first hug, a tentative look on his face. I stepped into his arms for a closer hug than Collin's, and my large cross-body purse wedged our lower bodies out farther than our upper. An email alert rang out on my phone inside my purse, causing it to vibrate against our bodies.

We stepped back from the clumsy encounter, brushing it off with awkward smiles to match the hug.

I slipped off my purse, fighting the urge to check my email before setting it under the table. What if it was Kiernan Moffat with the locket lady's contact info? Or had Gretta located the wreath? Or was it Simon Reese with more information on his grandma Eleanor Fitzsimmons? Why couldn't the email have come in ten minutes earlier? Because I'd have ended up at the restaurant without any makeup on and my hair a frizzy mess from the humidity.

"So how went the meeting with Kiernan Moffat today?" Collin asked. "Still a dodgy bloke, is he?"

Collin knew firsthand just how sketchy the man was due to his involvement with Valerie Burke, who'd attempted to kill his brother Aidan and steal his family's heirloom.

I recounted our visit with the appraiser and his clue about the woman with the other locket.

Collin's nose scrunched. "My granny has a locket with the hair plated on the outside. Thought it a bit mad, but sounds like it was common."

"Doesn't make it any less mad," Biddy said.

"But that's grand," Finn said. "Might turn out to be a great lead to finding your grandfather's family."

I smiled. "I hope so. Besides wanting to know the identity and relationship of the person in the pouch, work is piling up. Hope I'll have time to resume the DNA support group in the fall."

A surprised glint flashed in Finn's eyes. "Didn't think you'd be continuing the group after that last meeting. Was a bit brutal, wasn't it?"

I nodded. "Will give it one more shot."

Was he not planning on attending the meeting? Granted the last one had been a total soap opera, but Collin, Biddy, Finn, and I always stuck around after a meeting to hang out and have a pint. It was the one time Finn and I could count on seeing each other.

"So a week on Achill sounds brill," Collin said to Finn. "What are your plans?"

"When are you going to Achill?" I asked.

"In two weeks. My dad owns a cottage over there."

"That's right. He grew up in Galway," I said. "I visited the deserted village on Achill once with my grandma. Amazing." Except when I'd tripped on the uneven ground and tumbled down the hill until a stone building had stopped me. "So what are your plans?"

"Turns out we're both into kayaking."

My gaze narrowed. "On the ocean?" With my luck I'd end up in Iceland. I kayaked down a shallow river once and had to drag the kayak more than paddle it.

Finn laughed, nodding. "We'll stick to sea kayak routes. Will be grand. Get to see some sea caves and hopefully a few sharks and dolphins. Going to give abseiling a go also."

"What's that?" Biddy asked.

"Rappelling. Down the side of a cliff."

Collin's eyes widened. "Will be brilliant views."

Wouldn't be for me since I'd have my eyes shut. Yet I'd never do it in the first place.

"Once did that myself," Biddy said.

"When?" I asked.

"Actually, I climbed up the rocks, then rappelled back down." Biddy smiled proudly.

"Are you talking about that time at Tayto Park?"

Biddy nodded. "Was still rappelling."

Tayto Park was a kid's amusement park, not a thrill-seekers park for life-threatening adventures.

The corners of Collin's mouth curled into an amused smile, igniting a steamy gaze between him and Biddy. If they started playing footsie under the table, I was hauling Biddy to the bathroom and sticking her head in a sink of cold water.

Biddy's most serious relationship, right out of high school, had lasted four months. What if Biddy finally admitted she and Collin were in a relationship and it outlasted that one? I'd never had to compete with someone for Biddy's time.

"It's a controlled descent with an experienced coach," Finn said. "Will be grand making up for lost time with my dad." He gave me a grateful smile.

After thirty years of not knowing his biological father's identity, Finn had been thrilled to finally meet him. Thankfully, their story had a happy ending. I promised myself I wouldn't allow the discovery of my biological father's identity to change anything between Dad and me. Yet I hadn't even found the man, and I was debating attending the Murray reunion and spending quality time with Dad. Something I'd never have hesitated to do prior to receiving my DNA test results.

I had to go to the Murray reunion.

The waitress dropped off menus and took our drink orders. Collin and Finn chose whiskeys, while Biddy and I selected a French Bordeaux from an extensive wine list.

I inhaled a deep breath, perusing the menu. "Something smells delicious."

Finn's blue eyes peered over the top of his menu at me. "The specialty is lamb curry. Been looking forward to it all week."

My stomach tossed. Biddy shot me a not-so-discreet glance. I ignored it, but Finn didn't.

He quirked a brow. "You don't like curry or lamb?"

I shrugged it off. "Lamb's not my favorite."

"You bloody hate it," Biddy said.

I glared at Biddy. "I don't care for it." I turned to Finn. "But don't you dare not get it. Not like we're sharing a meal." Lamb was more popular in Ireland than in the Midwest, where I'd grown up. I had to get used to dining with those who ate it.

The waitress returned with our drinks, and Finn ordered the lamb. Finn ordering the dish bothered me more than usual. Was it because Pinky and I'd grown closer over the past months? Or because he'd ordered it despite knowing I detested it, even though I'd insisted he do so? I ordered sliced breast of chicken cooked in a Thai curry sauce with steamed rice to prove I liked curry. Not to mention the spice's strong scent would overpower the stench of lamb.

We enjoyed salads while chatting about summer plans. When the waitress delivered our entrees, I avoided looking at Finn's. Out of sight, out of mind. However, within five minutes the gamey smell of lamb caused my stomach to lurch. I tried not to inhale through my nose. Yet the lurching wouldn't stop. I excused myself to go to the bathroom.

I went to stand, and the heavy iron chair came with me, lifting a few inches off the floor. Nobody was looking, so I dropped back down in my seat. I felt behind me to discover that a belt loop on my jeans had somehow wrapped around a curved rod in the chair's fancy scroll design.

Finn's gaze narrowed on me. "Okay, are ya?"

I nodded, smiling, yet heat crept up my neck. I attempted to undo my button underneath the napkin on my lap, to help loosen the loop, but the waistband was pulled too tightly. My heart raced. I sucked in the deepest breath possible, inhaling the stench of lamb. My stomach tossed. I still couldn't unbutton my jeans. Sweat broke out on my upper lip. If I was going to be sick, should I throw up on the table or attempt to bolt for the bathroom while bent over lugging the heavy metal chair beneath my butt?

Biddy glanced over at me trying to readjust my seating to loosen the hold. "What are ya doing?" she muttered.

"I'm stuck," I whispered.

She peered at the back of my chair. "Janey, your belt loop is wrapped around the metal. How did you manage that?"

"Not on purpose, I guarantee you."

Concern creased Finn's brow. "What's wrong?"

My cheeks burned as I explained.

Finn and Collin came around the back of my chair to check it out. Nearby diners gave us curious stares, wondering how I was going to escape the chair. An older woman at the next table offered a small Hello Kitty sewing scissors from her purse.

"Think the lass will be needing a bigger one than that." Her husband flagged down a passing waitress, who returned with a scissors and handed it to Finn rather than Biddy.

Just shoot me now.

"I'll try cutting along the bottom seam so you can sew the loop back on," Finn said.

Just cut the freakin' thing off!

I nodded calmly. "Okay, thanks."

He cut the loop, freeing my too-tight jeans from the chair. I thanked him and fled to the bathroom. I splashed cold water on my face to stop the burning in my cheeks. I took several calming breaths and pulled my cell phone from my purse, wanting to escape into genealogy for a few peaceful moments. The earlier email was from Reverend Quinn with Duncan and Winifred MacDonald's marriage record and the woman's death record. Thankfully, the minister hadn't held Biddy's attempted bribe against me. I couldn't wait to get home and research. He also mentioned that the ladies packing up Duncan's belongings had set aside several photos for me, which he'd be happy to ship. Maybe the man's wife would resemble Grandpa. Gretta had also texted me an update that she'd searched sixteen cemeteries for the wreath and was still going strong.

The bathroom door swung open, almost hitting me. Biddy breezed into the tiny room.

"Are ya okay?"

I nodded. "As long as I don't get ill from the stench of lamb."

"Should've just been honest with the fella. He'd have ordered something else. Can't be starting a relationship based on lies."

"I was being polite. He'd been looking forward to it all week."

"So every time you're on a date and he orders lamb, you're going to sit in the bathroom until he finishes his meal?"

"No. And this isn't a date."

If this was a date, it had just outranked my worst date, previously held by Lucas Ferguson our senior year in high school. When my menu had caught fire from an open-flame candle centerpiece, he'd tossed his glass of water across the table. He'd overshot the burning menu, hitting my face and drenching my stylish hairdo. Disoriented, I'd dropped the burning menu, which had ignited the paper overlay on the tablecloth.

The rest was history.

As were Lucas and I after dating for three long months. I should have taken the menu and table going up in flames as a sign of our doomed relationship.

Maybe I should leave while I was ahead.

Ten minutes later, I wished I had.

"Where are you at with determining the connection between your grandpa and the man from Scotland?" Finn asked once I was safely seated at the table again.

"Right now Gretta is searching cemeteries for a wreath that Duncan MacDonald put on another grave. Should help me figure out the connection."

Finn's gaze darkened. "Gretta *Lynch*? The woman who nearly killed me and landed you in the A and E with a concussion?"

Biddy and Collin exchanged worried glances.

I nodded faintly. "Ah, yeah, it was never confirmed that I had a concussion."

"Well, it was confirmed that I almost died because of the bloody bitch." Finn's cheeks reddened, and he whipped his napkin onto the table.

I wanted to escape back into the bathroom. Finn saved me from having to do so, surging from his chair and stalking into the men's room. We all sat in silence.

"Janey," Biddy muttered. "Someone who dislikes the woman more than I do."

"I shouldn't have mentioned her name. But he's never talked about the accident or how much he obviously hates

Gretta." He apparently hadn't accepted the woman's apology.

"She nearly killed him. I'm sure he doesn't plan on inviting her over the holidays."

Finn exited the bathroom and headed toward the table. My heart went berserk. My breathing quickened. What if he demanded I stop having Gretta help with research? Could I honor his request? I felt a sense of pride having played a role in Gretta's transformation into a kinder person when assisting me three months ago with the Neil mystery.

Finn sat down, and before I could apologize, he did. "Sorry about that. Since the accident, sometimes I have a difficult time controlling my anger. Knowing the woman didn't intentionally try to kill me doesn't seem to make it much better." He took a drink of water.

"Have you thought about talking to someone, like a therapist?" I asked.

He'd never talked to me about it. We rarely saw each other. I saw Biddy daily, and I'd felt unqualified to help her overcome her fear of cemeteries. I wouldn't even know where to begin helping Finn with his PTSD.

"After tonight, I need to be looking into finding some help."

Biddy and I nodded, wearing sympathetic expressions.

Conversation was stilted for the remainder of dinner, and we skipped dessert and after-dinner drinks at the bar.

"We should be getting home," Biddy said. "Have an early train to Dublin to visit that mourning jewelry collector."

I was unsure if Biddy was coming to my rescue, ending the horrible evening, or if she had a booty call with Collin. Either way, I was thankful.

"We could meet up for drinks before I head back home," Finn said.

"Ah, yeah, sure." Why couldn't I have just bowed out gracefully with I was too busy solving my family mystery and I'd see him at the next DNA meeting in the fall? So if he wanted to see me again, it'd be up to him to attend.

Finn smiled. "Ah, grand."

Was it? What if the opportunity to make up for our first date didn't go off without a hitch? It certainly couldn't be any worse, could it?

Twelve

⁓

Upon arriving home, I made a cup of strong tea and threw my new jeans into the trash. Torching them in the woodstove would have entailed having the energy to walk out to the woodshed in the rain and getting drenched. I tried to forget about the embarrassing evening, which might cause even worse nightmares than Duncan MacDonald. I settled in on the couch with my cell phone and called Dad.

"I'm going with you to the reunion," I said.

"Ah, that's wonderful, Mags." The sparkle in his blue eyes and the happy dimple in his cheek came through in his voice. "It's being held at a castle outside Edinburgh. I already booked a double room."

"Wow. I've never stayed in a castle."

"And you won't have to look far for a cemetery. The place has its own."

"Omigod, a castle with a cemetery?"

"Yes. Every young girl's fairy-tale dream come true." He laughed.

"Well, since you hadn't mentioned it, now you know for

sure I'm going to spend quality time with my father rather than dead people." Speaking of dead people... I told him about finding Duncan MacDonald on my grandparents' graves and the man's intention of burying the mysterious purple-pouch person with them.

"I can't believe you didn't tell me this sooner, Mags. I could have come over. Are you okay?"

"I'm fine, and that's why I didn't tell you before. I knew you'd worry, and there's nothing to worry about. The man died of natural causes, so I'm just trying to determine their relationship to Grandpa." Easy peasy. Yeah, right.

Once I'd convinced my dad I wasn't traumatized for life, I promised to keep him updated on the mystery and to research sightseeing in the Edinburgh area. He gave me the name of the castle, and upon ending the call, I immediately pulled up the website.

The red-stone medieval structure boasting several rounded towers was situated on acres of wooded land just miles from Edinburgh. A gallery of photos provided a tour of the castle's four restaurants, full-service spa, archery grounds, and falconry facilities offering an owl, hawk, or falcon encounter. Not one photo of the cemetery. A bit disappointing, yet part of the exhilaration when entering an unfamiliar graveyard was the mystery of the unknown and what you might find.

The castle hosted weddings, meetings, and events. Guests could dine in the former dungeon or have afternoon tea in the library. Famous guests had included King Edward I, Sir Walter Scott, Oliver Cromwell, and Queen Victoria. I would be walking through the same halls as the former queen, who'd dressed in black and worn a mourning locket memorializing her husband for forty years!

I forced myself to close the website, needing to conduct genealogy research rather than vacation research. Yet my excitement over the castle took the edge off any anxiety about attending the Murray Clan reunion. For now.

I downloaded my raw DNA from Ancestry.com, which only took a minute. I then uploaded the DNA file to GEDmatch—a third-party genealogy website that allowed you to load your DNA from all major testing companies. If people took the extra step to join GEDmatch, hopefully they were serious about genealogical research. I'd been slammed with clients since the Roadshow episode, so I hadn't joined GEDmatch to further research Grandpa's family or my biological father. Tracing grandpa's ancestry, finding relations with the same locket, and determining the connection of Nancy Drew were now priorities. It would take twenty-four to forty-eight hours for my database of DNA matches to materialize.

Members in my DNA forums often discussed GEDmatch's nifty clustering program, which compared multiple matches and separated them into groups based on a shared ancestral line. Organizing my match list into groups would help me determine the most recent common ancestor that I shared with that cluster of people. In an ideal cluster world, I would have eight distinct clusters for my eight great-grandparents' lines. Once an ancestor or ancestral couple was identified, I could focus my research on that familial line or disregard it if not applicable to Grandpa's family.

I shot my second cousin Angie—Grandma's niece—an email asking if she could please upload her DNA from

Ancestry.com to GEDmatch if she didn't already have an account. That would enable me to cluster Flanagan matches and rule them out as Grandpa's relations.

I composed an email to Simon Reese, asking if his relations who'd tested would be willing to upload to GEDmatch. Genealogy wasn't as popular in England as it was in the States. And from my experience, the English tended to have greater privacy concerns than Americans. Hopefully, at least a few of his relatives would agree to register with GEDmatch. I needed as many known matches as possible in each cluster to help identify the shared family line. Not knowing my biological father was going to throw a wrench in the process. Out of my eight great-grandparents, four belonged to my father's lines.

I attached a photo of my locket to Simon's email. If his grandmother Eleanor was Grandpa's sister as I suspected, she might also have had a locket if the piece had memorialized one of their parents. I mentioned the dead woman's photo in the Belfast woman's locket. I also inquired if he had photos of his grandma that included possible siblings or parents so I could compare them to my photos and hopefully identify some of Grandpa's relations.

It had taken Simon three months to reply to my initial message, but he'd been much more responsive in recent communications. If I hadn't heard from him in three *days*, Biddy and I'd be hopping a ferry over to Cornwall.

I messaged our shared DNA matches. The three closest were still fairly distant. One hadn't signed into his account in over a year, and the other two had been one to three months. I described the locket and offered to email a photo, unable to attach one to Ancestry.com's messenger system. I made our family mystery sound intriguing and further enticed them with the promise of appearing on an episode of *Rags to Riches Roadshow*. If one of the matches was the Belfast woman who'd attempted to get on the show, she'd surely jump at the opportunity.

Fingers crossed.

I pulled up Reverend Quinn's email with (John) Duncan and Winifred MacDonald's marriage record and her death record, which also provided her birth year. The marriage record had Winifred's maiden name as Douglas, her father's name Bernard, and no mother's name. Unfortunately, it was the couple I'd located in Scotland's marriage index. The surname Douglas was still unfamiliar. Duncan's father was also Duncan MacDonald, and no mother's name. Typical, not giving the mother credit when she'd played the biggest role in the births of the children. No Collings or Fitzsimmons surnames, as I'd hoped. The couple had been married sixty-six years ago.

Now that I knew Winifred's exact death date, I could search for her obituary. And having her birth year, I could recheck possible birth records to determine her mother's maiden name, which might be the connection to my family. Winifred could have been a generation older than Grandpa. Even though a generation *averaged* twenty-five years, one sibling could have had her first child at age twenty, while a brother had his first at age fifty.

I added Duncan and Winifred MacDonald's information to my family tree as floaters—those not linked to anyone in the tree at this point. My number of floaters was quickly increasing. I added Winifred's obituary to my to-do list, unsure if the Isle of Bute had a paper or if it would have gone in a Glasgow one.

The doorbell rang.

I jumped, my heart going berserk.

Who'd be ringing my doorbell at midnight? Biddy? Doubtful. She'd likely headed straight to Collin's after dropping me off.

Thanks to the autopsy report that Duncan had died of natural causes, the coatrack wasn't blocking the front door. I crept through the mudroom and peeked out the door's small window to find an unfamiliar police officer and Gretta dressed in dark gray, her black hair hanging limp after undoubtedly having been caught in an earlier downpour. She held a large flashlight. I opened the door.

"Mags Murray?" the officer asked.

I nodded.

"Several concerned locals reported this woman skulking around the Knockbridge cemetery."

Gretta squared her shoulders, chin in the air. "I was not *skulking*. I was conducting important research."

"People are more than a wee bit worried about their loved ones' graves being robbed after what happened here in Ballycaffey. She claims to have been helping ya locate a grave."

I nodded. "She's assisting me with genealogy research."

"Hmph," Gretta muttered.

"People get too concerned, they'll also start selling off plots at Knockbridge, and I'll be holding you two responsible. Been attending Mass there since I was an altar boy, and my relations are buried there back four generations."

As if I could afford to be on another officer's radar as a troublemaker.

"Sorry about that. We'll stick to investigating during the day."

"Fine idea. 'Tisn't safe to be hanging out in graveyards at night. Can come across some dodgy characters. As you well know. And next time you mightn't have a shovel." He smirked.

A bit cheeky, wasn't he?

Had Garda Doherty also heard the Shovel Slayer rumor?

"I had nothing to do with that man's death. He had a heart attack. Ask the pathologist or the coroner."

I was going to demand a written note from them both stating that I was innocent. And have it laminated, since I feared my new nicknames might haunt me for years.

"Regardless, ya need to be a bit more careful."

The officer left, and Gretta came inside to wait for her husband. She didn't dare return to the cemetery to get her car and have the guards called once again.

Gretta thrust her phone at me. "Came across this in the twenty-third cemetery I visited. Think it's the arrangement we're looking for?"

The large wreath with artificial yellow and green flowers had a white ribbon with an Irish phrase written in cursive. The names on the grave were Lillian and Richard Flynn. No maiden name. What was the deal? You usually had a fairly good shot of people putting maiden names on older headstones. Grandma and I'd once come across a family plot with five headstones noting every women's maiden name. A gold mine. The surname Flynn didn't ring a bell. Once we confirmed this was Duncan's wreath, I could research the surrounding graves for possible relations. Along with the other Flynn graves in the cemetery.

"Hopefully, that's Irish for brother, sister, father, or some relation that will give me a clue."

"*In ár gcroíthe go deo* means in our hearts forever. Only came across a handful of decorations with Irish sayings in all the cemeteries. I bet this is it."

"Will have to ask Breeda Cullen to be sure."

"I can call in on her in the morning."

"Biddy and I can pop by on our way to the train station tomorrow. We have to follow up on a lead in Dublin." Goose bumps skittered across my skin at the thought of visiting Edgar Bates's mourning jewelry shop.

"If you'd like, I can go to the library and search for their obituaries and to the registrar's office for a marriage record. Her having died merely ten years ago, there might be some relations still in the area. I could ask around."

Gretta was quite enthusiastic and kind of infringing on my research territory. However, at least she was asking permission rather than taking it upon herself to do so. I could also use her help. Despite Finn's disapproval.

Was I choosing Gretta over Finn?

"That'd be great."

Headlights shone through the window as a vehicle pulled into the drive.

"I'll be right back. Thomas has an estimate for your conservatory." She returned with the detailed cost summary and left with a bounce in her step.

The cost was twice as much as my riding lawn mower and fuel tank. I'd have to deal with looking out foggy windows until I knew if I'd be paying for a cremation and burial in the near future.

I watched Tommy and Gretta's car lights disappear into

the night. Maybe the woman had been a total witch because she'd needed a sense of purpose. Gretta was in her late seventies. Grandma Moses, the American Folk artist, had embarked on her career at the age of seventy-eight. My mom had always insisted that I needed to find a stable career or go to college, like my sisters had. That working seasonal jobs would get me nowhere in life. I'd mentioned my mother's concern to Grandma, and she'd told me the inspirational story about Grandma Moses. When I'd shared the example with Mom, she'd replied, "You don't want to be another Grandma Moses. Find yourself now. What's the chance you'll live to be a hundred and one or even seventy-eight?"

A good thing my mom had never pursued a career as a motivational speaker.

Thirteen

"CAN'T BE sure if that's the same wreath." Breeda Cullen barely glanced at the photo while clearing a breakfast table in the cozy conservatory. "I didn't be getting much of a look at it. Unlike the couple who mentioned it the other day."

"Are they still here?" I asked.

She frowned, grabbing a basket of brown bread from a table. "They've checked out. Sorry I can't be of more help." She headed to the kitchen, carrying a tray of dirty dishes.

"In an awfully big hurry to get rid of us, I'd say," Biddy whispered. "Not offering us tea or even a bloody biscuit."

I nodded, admiring the spotless conservatory windows providing a clear view of the colorful garden. Someday.

We headed outside.

"She'd been so intrigued by the case the other day," I said. "You'd think she'd have wanted an update. Not like she was in the middle of preparing a full Irish breakfast for a dozen guests. Dirty dishes weren't going anywhere."

As we pulled out of the drive, a small blue car pulled in.

The man behind the wheel gave us a wave, as did the woman in the passenger seat.

"Wasn't that the wreath couple?" I said.

"Certainly was." Biddy put the car in reverse and backed up the drive as the people stepped from their vehicle.

I showed them the picture of the wreath on my phone.

The woman smiled at it. "Ah yes, that's the same lovely wreath, isn't it, luv?"

Her husband nodded. "Certainly is. *In ár gcroíthe go deo.* In our hearts forever."

"I'm so glad we caught you," I said. "Thought you'd checked out."

"Oh my, I hope not," the woman said. "Haven't packed our luggage and have plans in the area tomorrow."

The couple headed inside.

I peered through the conservatory windows at Breeda sitting at a table, sipping a cup of tea. "Why did the woman lie to us?"

"And now has time for a spot of tea after racing around cleaning when we were trying to chat with her."

Biddy and I headed back inside to the conservatory.

Breeda managed a strained smile.

"What great timing," I said. "We met up with the couple as they were coming in. They identified the wreath."

Breeda began reorganizing the tea bags currently sorted by flavor. "Guess I was confused. Must have been the other couple that checked out this morning."

Biddy and I exchanged skeptical looks.

"Why are you lying?" I asked.

Breeda frowned, fidgeting with the tea bag in her hand. "I'm sorry. It's just that the man's death has been bad for business. Tourists and locals have been coming 'round taking snaps of the house where the grave robber stayed. Starting to get a reputation. Afraid it'll be scaring away potential guests." She heaved a sigh. "Lost my husband, Andrew, almost ten years ago this autumn. Can't afford to be losing my business." She slapped a hand over her mouth, capturing a sob. Tears flowed down her red blotchy cheeks, and she blew her nose with a napkin.

"Don't you feel like a right eejit?" Biddy said to me.

Me? She'd agreed Breeda was acting fishy.

Biddy comforted the distraught woman while I poured her a fresh cup of tea. I'd definitely be more careful in the future before interrogating someone to tears.

The Dublin jeweler—a tall, thin older man in a dark suit—unclasped the top of his ornate gold ring to reveal a stranger's lock of woven gray hair behind beveled glass. Biddy cringed next to me, no doubt wanting to torch the place with the bundles of sage in her purse. I pressed my lips firmly together to prevent the top one from curling up to my nose. Surprisingly, Edgar Bates's nails were well manicured and not long and yellow like I'd imagined. However, he had mourning rings on four fingers. His dimly lit shop was located street level rather than in the dark recesses of an abandoned building's basement. Yet it smelled faintly like a musty attic where sellers had discovered their heirlooms boxed up for decades. On the fringe of a rather sketchy part of town meant more affordable rent, since mourning jewelry wasn't flying out of the packed display cases I'd been trying to ignore.

"The Victorians believed hair contained the essence of the person and symbolized immortality," the man said in an English accent. "It was used to create everything from exquisitely detailed scenes in jewelry to memorial artwork." He gestured behind him at a framed vintage photo of a young woman on the wall. A floral design weaved from dark hair decorated the white matting. "Mourners would often send the dead to their graves after giving them one last haircut." He snipped his fingers in the air. "Frequently, the hair was plaited and pressed into lockets, which were then worn close to the heart."

"And my mum thought *I* was odd asking her to pull fifteen strands of hair from a dead man for DNA evidence," Biddy said.

The man looked like Biddy's idea was crazier than his entire morbid collection. He turned to me. "Seeing as your grandfather possessed the locket, he quite likely acquired it from his mother, who'd received it as a memorial from one of her parents. Otherwise, as a man, he'd have been given a ring or cufflinks. However, spouses were sometimes also given a memento, in which case it could have come from either family line."

I gestured to my locket, displayed on the jeweler's red velvet tray on the glass case. "Do you think the floral design engraved on the front might be a family crest?"

He shook his head. "It was likely the deceased initials."

Initials? How hadn't I realized that before?

Excitement zipped through me as he traced a finger over the engraving and cursive letters took form where I'd previously seen flowers.

"V...L...E," he muttered.

I squinted at the last loopy letter. "Could that possibly be a *C* rather than an *E*?" Like for Collings?

He shrugged. "Perhaps. Based on the deceased's hairstyle and dress in that other woman's locket, I was able to estimate the date of death as..." He closed his eyes, as if conjuring up the dead woman's appearance. His eyes shot open, startling Biddy and me. "June 1898."

"Wow," Biddy muttered. "Can you be guessing my birthdate?"

His gaze narrowed. "I was merely jesting. If I could pinpoint a photo's date down to an exact month within a year, I'd surely be using that skill to fill auditoriums." He brushed off Biddy's disappointed look. "I recall the year 1898 was engraved on her locket, seeing as it was the year my beloved grandmother passed away. The jewelry was most often inscribed with the dearly departed's year of death and possibly a few words of comfort." He took a small tweezers from a drawer and opened the locket, revealing my grandparents' photos. "May I?"

I nodded, unsure what he was asking permission to do.

Using the tweezers, he carefully pulled back the top corner of my grandpa's photo. He placed a small lighted magnifier to an eye and studied the gold piece. A smile curled the corners of his mouth. "What a find indeed. The year is legible—1898."

My heart raced. "So it must be the same locket as that woman's in Belfast."

"I would presume so."

"My grandpa was born in 1922, so the necklace couldn't have been a memorial to his mother. Maybe she'd passed it down to him. Do you recall the deceased's approximate age in the photo?"

He shrugged. "A bit difficult to gauge. When the *dead* are at rest, the serene look on their faces always takes years off their *lives*." He chuckled at his morbid humor.

I managed a feeble smile.

He returned to the locket. "And the jeweler's mark is WAT—Wright, Aldridge, and Turner. A very prestigious jeweler in Birmingham, England, well into the 1940s."

To think I'd been wearing the clues all this time. I typed the details into the notepad on my cell phone.

I could search the Birmingham death records for women with the initials VLE or VLC who'd died in 1898. There couldn't be more than...several dozen. My enthusiasm faded. Who was to say the family had even resided in the area? Maybe the rich and famous came from all over England to have their mourning jewelry crafted by this prestigious jeweler. Had Grandpa's family possibly moved from Birmingham to the Isle of Bute?

"Would have been an affluent family with such a jeweler," he said.

Biddy perked up next to me. "See, that key on the chain *is* to a treasure chest or trunk filled with family jewels."

I couldn't imagine Grandpa having come from a wealthy family when Grandma once mentioned he'd never owned more than three pairs of pants or two pairs of shoes at one time. They'd shared one vehicle for twenty-five years. Luckily, it wasn't my current car.

"Fancy mourning jewelry wouldn't have been nearly as common in Ireland, with all the deaths and poverty during the Victorian era. Sadly, the country didn't recover from the famine until many years later."

"What would you appraise it at?"

He quirked an intrigued brow. "Are you interested in selling?"

I shook my head. "Would like an estimated value in case it's ever stolen again."

"Not having a photo or lock of hair makes it less collectible. However, the inside engravings still being legible would definitely help... I'd say three thousand euros. Of course, the value depends on supply and demand at the time."

I peered down at the case filled with mourning jewelry. High supply and low demand.

Biddy blew out a low whistle. "What if Mags were to put a clump of her hair and a photo of a dead lady off the internet in the locket? How much more would it be worth?"

The man sneered at Biddy. "Surely you jest. The *deceased's* hair was sacred."

An older, refined-looking gentleman in a suit entered the shop. Edgar Bates gave the man a wave and promised to be with him momentarily.

"I'd be more than happy to share a photo of the locket with other collectors. One of them may have come across the piece at some point. I took a photo of the other lady's necklace but failed to request her contact information. I'm even having difficulty recalling her name. Memory is not what it used to be." He snapped a shot of my locket, and I removed it from the red velvet tray. "If I come across the other photo, I shall let you know."

We left the shop, squinting back the bright sunlight,

sucking in deep cleansing breaths. Despite having been shrouded in death for the past half hour, I felt invigorated, excited about the new clues I had uncovered.

Biddy whisked out her juniper sage spray instead of lighting up the sage bundle in her purse. "Wish I had a scouring pad to scrub my skin off."

She swept the spray up and down the length of us several times, causing me to inhale the overpowering woodsy scent. I began coughing, my eyes watering. So much for the deep cleansing breaths. Passersby shot us concerned looks until I managed to get my coughing attack under control.

"To think your grandpa may have come from a wealthy family, rich enough to hand out costly gifts to family and friends attending the funeral. Then you have someone like poor Duncan MacDonald, who couldn't even afford to bury a loved one. Bet that made him a bit resentful and was why he stole the necklace."

"Being a genealogist, my grandma had to have found the history of this locket interesting. Why didn't she share the story with me? Or at least mention it'd had been passed down in my grandpa's family?"

Because being a genealogist myself, she knew I'd have used the locket to trace Grandpa's family? Grandma had believed everyone had the right to know the truth about their ancestry.

Except for me?

Upon arriving back in Ballycaffey, we stopped at McCarthy's pub for a pint and a quick pizza. I needed to get home and research women with the initials VLE and VLC who'd died in 1898 in the Birmingham area. Actually, in the entire country of England...and possibly Wales and Scotland.

My two buddies were there playing darts. Before they could raise their pints and blurt out more nicknames, I told them the autopsy confirmed the man had died of a heart attack.

The guy in a *Fear the Deere* T-shirt gave me a sympathetic smile. "Now don't be blaming yerself, lass, for causing the fella's heart attack. Shouldn't have been digging up the grave in the first place."

His friend nodded. "Aye, not yer fault the fella had a heart condition and ye scared the life out of him."

I couldn't win.

Biddy told her mom Edgar Bates's story about the Victorian tradition of crafting the deceased's hair into jewelry and artwork. "So I'd be needing fifteen strands of that Duncan MacDonald's hair to be weaving into a lovely piece of art."

Ita rolled her eyes. "And I'd be liking a daughter who doesn't pull hair from dead men's heads and hangs out with the sorts that collect dead people's jewelry. Not to mention, you nearly failed your art class in school." She headed down the bar to refill drinks and likely pour herself one.

My phone dinged the arrival of an email. Simon Reese. I anxiously scanned his message.

"My cousin Simon loaded his DNA to GEDmatch, so it should hit my database in the next day or two. He sounds intrigued about the locket. His grandma hadn't been the sentimental sort, so if she'd had a locket, she'd likely sold it. Like she had most of their family photos. Great. No photos to compare to the ones in my family albums to help identify

Grandpa's relations. He says in talking to his mother he discovered his grandma was born on the Isle of Bute but then moved to England. He's not sure at what age." I let out a frustrated groan. "Where in England? Birmingham, Cornwall..."

"Cornwall is a big bloody difference from the Isle of Bute. Like several hundred miles."

I collapsed against the back of the barstool and took several gulps of cider. While I was responding to Simon's email asking if he knew of any family ties to Birmingham, Gretta entered the pub.

The John Deere guy playing darts paused his hand in midair, and conversations ceased. All eyes were on Gretta. I pulled her up a stool to end the awkward situation. It was likely the first time she'd ever set foot in McCarthy's pub. Guess picking up road rubbish had brought her down to the level of us commoners.

Gretta ordered a tea. She wasn't as perky as the night before, when she'd nearly been arrested for cemetery vagrancy. She removed a piece of paper from her purse and handed me Lillian Flynn's and Richard Flynn's obituaries.

She frowned. "No children's names or other relations are listed in either. About all hers says is that she was a brilliant weaver who'd won loads of awards for her wool creations. He was raised in Roscommon, so would guess he's the possible connection to your family, seeing as she was from Birmingham."

"Birmingham?" Biddy and I both blurted out.

Gretta nodded.

"That's interesting, isn't it now?" Biddy said.

Gretta quirked a curious brow. "Thought our dead fella was from the Isle of Bute?"

Biddy's gaze narrowed on Gretta. *Our* dead fella?

I filled Gretta in on the locket's manufacturer in Birmingham, leaving out our lesson on mourning jewelry.

I smiled. "This is an incredible find. I have no clue what exactly the connection is, but there must be one." Had Lillian Flynn been the reason Grandpa settled in Ireland's Midlands? If she was born in 1918 in Birmingham, she could have been his older sibling, or possibly a first cousin.

"I can visit the registrar's office tomorrow. They weren't accepting record requests today. I'll collect the couple's marriage record to confirm her maiden name. And maybe her death record would give her birth date, not merely the year."

Even if we didn't figure out Lillian Flynn's maiden name, knowing she was from Birmingham was huge.

Biddy's body went rigid. "Thanks for the offer, but I can be doing that."

"I don't feel right starting a project and not seeing it through."

Biddy gave Gretta a tight smile. "You're grand. I'll take it from here."

The woman's cold gaze narrowed on Biddy. "If I fancy a visit to the registrar's office, I think I'll be doing so."

Biddy held her gaze. "Let's ask Mags who she'd be preferring to go to the office."

Their gazes darted to me.

"Seriously?" I said.

Biddy was my best friend and sidekick. Yet I didn't want to be the one responsible for Gretta morphing back into an evil witch and the entire town blaming me. Besides, it made me feel good to have helped Gretta find a sense of purpose. Maybe I'd inspired her to be the next Grandma Moses.

My email app dinged. A welcome interruption. I read the appraiser's message.

"Kiernan Moffat found the paperwork for the woman with the locket, Michelle Thompson. She was fine with him giving me her contact information. Hopefully, I'll be making a road trip to Portaferry, County Down, near Belfast tomorrow."

Gretta smiled brightly. "I could be going with ya, seeing as I won't be having any research to conduct."

A wild look seized Biddy's face, and she appeared ready to spring from the stool and take Gretta down.

"Thanks, but if you could go to the registrar's office, that'd be great," I said.

Biddy shot Gretta a victorious grin. Why was Biddy being so competitive and against Gretta helping out when Biddy had to work tomorrow anyway? This was getting too weird. As if I had time to be playing referee. It was situations like this that made me prefer hanging out with dead people rather than the living.

I flew home to contact Michelle Thompson from County Down. Kiernan Moffat had only provided her email, no address or phone number. Not that I couldn't find both in a matter of minutes on the internet. Yet if the woman recalled not having given either to the appraiser, I might come off a bit stalkerish, especially if I showed up at her door. I kept the message short, attached a photo of my locket, and crossed my fingers. The opportunity to appear on the *Rags to Riches Roadshow* would likely get her to respond.

My DNA matches were now available on GEDmatch. Thousands of them, but not many close ones, such as Simon Reese or Grandma's niece Angie—who hadn't yet replied to my email. Not one of the top five hundred matches had the surname Flanagan, Collings, or Fitzsimmons. Many people merely used initials or cutesy nicknames like Sherlock Bones, which made me laugh despite my frustration. At least users were required to provide email addresses. However, I often found people provided invalid ones to prevent being contacted. A small tree icon next to a member's profile name indicated the person had supplied a family tree. Less than 5 percent of my matches had one. Since I couldn't cluster until I had several close *known* ancestor matches, I held off for now.

You could join GEDmatch projects based on criteria such as surnames and geographic locations that enabled you to connect with those matches conducting similar research. I submitted requests for England, Ireland, and Scotland projects. England was broken down into numerous regions, like the West Midlands, including Birmingham. No project for the Isle of Bute, so I selected Argyll. The island was a part of the Argyll and Bute council area. I joined Westmeath, Meath, Donegal, Cork, and the other top locations my ancestors hailed from, according to my 23andMe DNA test. There were no projects for Fitzsimmons, Collings, Flynn, or Douglas, so I joined one for MacDonald. I couldn't imagine it was Duncan MacDonald who I was related to, but he and Winifred might have had children. Different members ran each project, so approval response times would vary for the twenty-two I signed up for.

The Ireland projects should also bring me one step closer to identifying my biological father.

One of my three DNA matches with Simon had responded to my message, anxious to learn more about the family mystery and to appear on TV. She failed to answer my question about having a similar locket, which made me assume that was the first she'd heard about it.

I began researching the initials and death year on my locket. It was hard to say if the first initial, *V*, was for the woman's legal name or nickname. Her middle name would most likely not be on the death record. I assumed the initial for the last name, *C* or *E*, was her married name. The UK government records site wouldn't allow me to search by merely a surname's first initial or first few letters. I found a list of the top one hundred most common surnames in 1900 England and was checking off those starting with a *C* or *E*. There were a few deaths with variations of Collings in Birmingham, but none with a first name beginning with *V*. When I expanded that to all of England, a slew came up, several with the first initial *V*.

Too overwhelmed to search without more details, such as the woman's age, I added the initials to the tree as Grandpa's grandmother from Birmingham. None of which I knew was accurate.

Yet I had the feeling that *VLE* slash *VLC* held the *key* to my family mystery.

Fourteen

THE FOLLOWING MORNING, I checked my GEDmatch account while gulping down a double-bagged cup of tea. Still no close DNA matches, but I'd been approved for numerous projects, including several Ireland counties and also Scottish ones near the Isle of Bute. Most importantly, Birmingham, England. My ancestors' hot spot. I anxiously ran a report to identify matches in the West Midlands-slash-Birmingham project. Several dozen appeared. I clicked the button to cluster them into groups based on our shared ancestor lines.

The doorbell rang.

I growled in frustration. My doorbell rang more now than when I was growing up and bored friends would pop over to hang out or go for a bike ride.

My annoyance vanished when I saw Rosie's smiley face peering through the door's window. I invited her inside for tea.

"Thanks a mil, but I can only be staying a moment. On the way to my hairdresser. Hope it's not too early to call in, but my brother Albert received information on the woman who sold the locket to the shop in Edinburgh. Her name was Harriett Neely. The shop owner is contacting her to get the okay to share her email with you."

"Neely doesn't ring a bell, but most surnames haven't lately. Possibly her married name." I couldn't keep track of all the names floating around in my head. "I hope her email address is still valid, since she moved to Australia."

"I hope I didn't seem too pushy about you holding a wake for that fella. I didn't mean I thought ya should feel obligated. Just if you did, I'd be happy to alter his suit to a proper fit."

I smiled. "If I end up having one, that'd be very sweet of you."

"I haven't been to a wake in some time. Felt awful having missed Maggie's on account of the flu bug. If you don't hold a wake, Edmond and I'd be happy to attend the funeral so it doesn't appear the fella was without friends or family. Always feel so badly when a funeral has low attendance."

Talking about burials reminded me of Rosie's daughter-in-law Stella, her son Sean's widow. In the course of questioning Stella about Finn's car accident, I'd learned that she had no plans to retire in the Connollys' white bungalow, which was surrounded by acres of family land passed down for generations. She also likely had no desire to be buried in the plot next to her husband.

"I'm not sure if you're aware that Stella plans to retire in the Canary Islands."

Rosie braced a hand on the back of the love seat, the color draining from her light-pink cheeks. "I hadn't a clue."

I ushered the poor woman over to the couch to sit before she fainted on the floor.

"It had been my son Sean's wish that she inherit the family land once I was gone. He certainly couldn't have known she'd intended to sell it off to purchase a home in the Canary Islands." The color returned to her cheeks, now a bright red rather than pink. "Of course she had no plans of telling me this. Never liked that woman. Sean could have done much better."

I didn't want to taint her son's memory by telling her that he may have indeed done better, since he'd been quite the womanizer.

"I'm sorry I didn't tell you sooner. When I learned of her plans, you and I'd just met, and I didn't think it was my place to meddle in family business. And then later I forgot. Just thought of it now while we were discussing burial plots. I'm guessing she doesn't plan on being shipped back to Ireland to be buried. I hope with the selling frenzy that she hasn't already sold off her plot." I wouldn't want some strangers buried in my family plot. Precisely why I was so determined to learn if Duncan or Nancy Drew were related to me.

Rosie shook her head in disgust. "She most certainly hasn't sold it. She doesn't yet have the rights to it. And now she never will." The woman surged from the couch. "I'll be calling in on her after my appointment."

"Again, I'm so sorry."

"I can't thank you enough for telling me, luv." A smile put a twinkle in the woman's eyes, and she slipped a warm hand around mine, giving it a gentle squeeze. "It means so much that you cared enough to tell me."

After Rosie left, I resumed clustering the West Midlands-slash-Birmingham project. Several colorful squares material-ized on a graph. A large purple one at the top. Nearly 50 percent of the matches had family trees, versus merely 5 percent of my overall matches. That was a good sign that members who joined projects were more serious researchers. I clicked open the tree for my closest match. Our most recent common ancestor was likely second great-grandparents.

My phone dinged the arrival of a text. Gretta.

Lillian Flynn's maiden name was Drummond.

Drummond was the mother's maiden name on the birth record for the Henry Collings born on the Isle of Bute the same date as Grandpa. It was also one of Grandpa's middle names. More evidence that the Isle of Bute's Henry was indeed my grandpa Henry Liam. If Duncan MacDonald had placed a wreath on a Drummond relation's grave, then Lillian had most likely been Grandpa's cousin. Had other Drummonds lived in the area? Had Grandpa moved here to be near his mother's relations? Was his mother, Catherine, possibly buried here?

I searched for a Lillian Drummond born 1918 in Birmingham and discovered England's online birth index was only available prior to 1916. Knowing what other Drummonds were buried in the same cemetery as Lillian would be helpful. It was a more concrete clue and time better spent than searching for a dead woman with the initials *VLE* or *VLC*. Or perusing GEDmatch family trees unsure what I was even looking for, hoping something would jump out at me.

I was off to the Knockbridge cemetery.

Fifteen minutes later, I was pulling up in front of a rural church adjacent to a newer cemetery on the outskirts of

Knockbridge. Unlike Ballycaffey's cemetery, the graves were laid out in an orderly fashion without weathered stones and Celtic crosses on treacherous terrain at the back.

I made a beeline toward the Flynns' grave based on Gretta's directions. I encountered an elderly couple placing flowers on a grave and took their friendly smiles as a green light welcoming conversation. Unfortunately, they weren't there visiting any Drummonds, Flynns, or other familiar surnames. And they hadn't known Lillian or Richard Flynn. I thanked them and moved on. It was worth a shot.

Grandma had always struck up a conversation with cemetery visitors unless they appeared too distraught or to need privacy. On a weekend when the cemeteries were busy, it could take her hours to make her way through one. It was like her coffee hour or happy hour, socializing with others at cemeteries. She'd once met an English gent visiting a Ballycaffey grave near our family plot. Turned out he was a distant relative of her Flanagans.

Lillian and Richard Flynn had an impressive granite stone with a white urn on each side for fresh flowers. Apparently, the Flynns had expected fairly regular visitors to bring flowers, meaning they likely had family in the area. Grandpa? The current flowers were too wilted for Duncan MacDonald to have placed them there. Besides, why would he have brought flowers when he'd had a wreath? A *lovely* green-and-yellow floral wreath with Irish written on a white ribbon.

A lovely wreath that was no longer there.

Had thieves now resorted to stealing cemetery decorations? I peered around at neighboring graves in case the cemetery caretaker had moved the wreath while mowing and had forgotten to replace it. Most graves had flowers, fairy statues, or figurines, but not the Flynns' wreath. If other decorations were still intact, it was unlikely a cemetery thief had swiped the wreath.

Then who had stolen it and why?

I ran to the back of the church and removed the garbage can lid. The stench of rotting food and several flies overwhelmed me. No wreath. I raced through the cemetery, making sure somebody hadn't stolen the wreath to place on another grave. A miniature Christmas tree was once stolen from Grandpa's grave. Grandma and I'd found it on Peter Dunphy's grave. We'd gone home and filled a tin with coal and driven straight to Agnes Dunphy's house. Without a word Grandma had handed the guilty-looking woman the coal and left.

My phone's email chimed. Michelle Thompson. I quickly read her message.

She'd love to meet in person to share her family photos and research. She was available later today or one day next week. No way was I waiting until next week. Portaferry, Down, located in Northern Ireland, was a three-hour drive. Leaving now would put me there midafternoon. If our visit lasted into the night, I could get a hotel room. I responded that I'd be there in three hours.

Having finished checking all the graves, I bolted from the cemetery and toward my car. Biddy was working, so I had no wingman. I had to admit, even though it irked me when she played the working-part-time card, it was nice having a partner. Someone to bounce ideas off and to share the driving on the six-hour road trip. However, if I told her that, she might quit her job to be my assistant.

Lately, a mystery needed solving about every three

months. And although the case of the Neils' manuscript was an exception, I generally wasn't paid. So the rest of the time she'd have to assist me with genealogy research. I loved Biddy to death, but that would be too much togetherness. And despite having perseverance and great mystery-solving skills, she wouldn't make a great genealogist. She was horrible at remembering dates and names—unless it involved TV or movie celebrities or characters, except for Dougal McGuire. She was just starting to overcome her fear of cemeteries. And she lacked the required focus...er, obsession...to perform mental gymnastics while researching into the wee hours of the morning.

Yet I still wished she had the day off.

Fifteen

PORTAFERRY WAS a village an hour south of Belfast. It was located at the southern tip of the Ards Peninsula, where a narrow strait connected the Irish Sea with a large lake. Michelle Thompson's kitchen window provided a spectacular view of fishing boats sailing out to sea like my grandfather might have done when traveling fifty or so miles across to Scotland to visit family. Upon reaching Scotland you could sail north along the shoreline to the Isle of Bute, situated on the waterway leading into the port of Glasgow. The island's close proximity had me wanting to charter a fishing boat to take me there. However, having tea with Grandpa's first known relative was even better than exploring Bute's cemeteries.

Michelle set chocolate-covered biscuits on the table next to the tea service. The thirtyish-year-old blond woman was dressed in jeans and a lightweight cream-colored wool sweater. Despite being the middle of summer, a cool breeze blew in off the sea. A bit cool for my white capris and jean jacket.

"My granny Delia was the daughter of Elizabeth Collings, whose parents were William Collings and Victoria Fitzsimmons."

Fitzsimmons? My heart raced.

"My grandpa Liam's last name was Fitzsimmons. However, I believe he was born on the Isle of Bute, Scotland, to a Henry Collings and Catherine Drummond."

Michelle nodded. "Henry was Elizabeth's older brother. She had two that I'm aware of. However, I didn't find much on their brother Walter. I would guess your grandpa's name Liam was a nickname for William, his grandfather."

"Never thought about that being a nickname for William. Liam was his middle name, and Henry was his first."

The family names started to fall into place.

"I contacted England's General Registrar's Office with estimated marriage years for the three siblings. I received a copy of the records for Elizabeth and Henry, but not Walter. Henry Collings had indeed married a Catherine Drummond."

Yes! I wanted to surge from my chair, punching a celebratory fist in the air over finally having confirmed that Henry Collings, born in 1922 on the Isle of Bute, was without a doubt my grandpa!

Perched on the edge of the chair, I smiled and asked, "Where were they married?"

"Birmingham in 1916. Same place Elizabeth and Henry were born." She handed me my great-grandparents' marriage record.

No wonder I hadn't been able to find Henry and Catherine's marriage in the *Scottish* records online index. The UK vital records site didn't include marriages. You had to contact the registrar's office directly, as Michelle did, and wait weeks for a copy of the record, if it even existed. You might luck out and find the record in "select" English marriages in other research sites databases.

The document noted that Henry had worked at the Post Office Savings Bank at Blythe House, his address, and that his father, William Collings, was a banker. Catherine Drummond's father, Andrew, owned a pub. Amazing how one piece of paper provided me with the most background I had on Grandpa's family.

I filled Michelle in on Simon's grandmother Eleanor Fitzsimmons having moved from the Isle of Bute to southern England at some point. "With my grandfather also having the last name Fitzsimmons, I'm guessing he was raised by the same family, likely a relative of Victoria's."

"I didn't come across a connection to Fitzsimmons in that area. However, I had to put my research aside for personal reasons a few months after I attended the *Rags to Riches Roadshow* filming in Belfast. This will certainly inspire me to get back at it. I'd love to help in any way I can. I found the Collings family in the 1911 census at the address on both Henry's and Elizabeth's marriage records." She handed me a copy of the census with handwritten notes. William was born in Manchester and worked in finance. "William's wife, Victoria Fitzsimmons, came from a very wealthy family in banking. Might be how William got into the family business or how the couple met. Their address was in a prestigious area."

I shook my head in disbelief. "You never would have known my grandpa came from money."

Michelle shrugged. "He might not have. Not sure what happened with the family money. After my great-grand-mother Elizabeth's first husband died, she married a mariner from Belfast and lived a quiet and unpretentious life here in Portaferry, never passing along her family history. Her husband was Catholic and she was Protestant, so she'd possibly been disowned by her family, which would explain the lack of oral history. Religion did, and still does, divide many families in Northern Ireland and the Republic."

"Did you ever come across info on the family in Scotland?"

"Sorry. I didn't." She placed a slightly faded black-and-white photo on the table in front of me. "That's Elizabeth and my granny Delia in her early twenties. Not sure about the others. There's no names or date on the back."

My grandpa's happy eyes smiled back at me, just a bit older than he'd been in his graduation photo in my locket. So Elizabeth's family was likely who Grandpa had visited on his trips to Belfast.

I slipped the locket from my purse and showed Michelle Grandpa's photo. "I'd say the gentleman next to your grandma is her first cousin, my grandpa."

Michelle smiled wide. "Ah, brilliant. I'd certainly say so. Quite a handsome fella, he was."

Elizabeth was tall with a classic 1940s hairstyle and wearing a polka-dot dress. Her daughter Delia was merely a shorter version of her mother and also dressed in polka dots. The other five in the photo—three girls and two boys, including Grandpa—appeared close in age, early to mid-twenties. The girls had longer dark hair and wore knee-length dresses—two patterned and one polka dot. Polka dots appeared to have been the rage at the time. Everyone was dressed up as if attending a wedding or special event.

"I wonder if the others might be his siblings," I said. "Do you mind if I take a picture of it to send to our relation in Cornwall, see if one might be his grandma, Eleanor?"

"You can have that copy. I had several made for a family gathering a few years ago. It's an extra."

I smiled at my first photo of Grandpa's family.

"Sadly, I don't have any photos of Elizabeth's parents, except for the one of Victoria in my locket."

She slipped the top off a small white box on the table and removed a necklace identical to mine. My breath caught in my throat as she unclasped the heart-shaped locket, revealing a yellowed black-and-white photo of our ancestor Victoria Fitzsimmons on one side and a woven lock of her silver hair behind beveled glass on the other. Eyes closed, she looked at peace. I couldn't recall having seen a photo of the woman in Grandma's album. My heart ached for a bereaved William, or other family member, distributing the memorial jewelry to family and possibly friends. How many more lockets were out there?

"Can take a snap of it if you'd like," Michelle said.

It was a bit creepy, yet incredible, to have a photo of my second great-grandmother, dead or alive. I snapped a picture. I'd have to be extra careful not to accidentally text it to Finn. At least the last photo of a dead person I'd sent him had been of the man's back rather than the eerie expression on his face. A look that might haunt me until I joined my grandparents in our family plot.

"If Elizabeth and Henry had at least one brother, there must be another locket out there," I said. "I know of one that belonged to a woman now in Australia. I hope to reach out to her. Edgar Bates said jewelry may have also been given to the spouses, so I suppose that'd make sense. Maybe my necklace had been Catherine's, Henry's wife."

Michelle nodded. "Edgar Bates was quite an interesting fella, wasn't he?"

"Certainly was."

"So glad Kiernan Moffat reached out to me. He also mentioned featuring our family story on an upcoming episode." She appeared a bit starstruck by the appraiser. Best if I didn't fill her in on the dodgy man. "To think, we might never have connected if it hadn't been for the off chance that Kiernan had seen us both wearing identical lockets. How mad is that?"

I nodded. "Kind of freaky."

"Will be interesting to see where it all leads us."

Michelle agreed to load her DNA to GEDmatch pronto and to resume her research after she finished up a work project the next week. I promised to keep her updated on my findings. Now, knowing who I was looking for and how the Collings and Fitzsimmons surnames fit into the puzzle would make research much easier.

I sat in Michelle's driveaway and typed up an email to Simon Reese, hoping he'd respond by the time I got home. I filled him in on my visit and my discovery of Victoria Fitzsimmons. I asked if his grandma had possibly taken the last name of relatives who might have raised her and likely my grandpa. Had the children's parents, Henry and Catherine, died, so they'd gone to live with relations? Had Grandpa moved from Birmingham to the Isle of Bute down to Cornwall, then to

Ireland? That would have been a lot of moving around for a young boy.

Who knew for sure? All I *did* know was that I had to start driving home while trying to maintain the speed limit despite my excitement to start researching. I had a feeling that tonight my grandpa's family mystery would be solved.

Sixteen

I studied the 1919 black-and-white photo on my laptop. The distinguished-looking gentleman in a black bowler hat, with a scarf wrapped around his neck and tucked into a dark wool jacket, had his chin jutted out in defiance. He was five foot nine with blue eyes, a thick dark mustache, and a polished complexion except for a scar by his left ear. Those were the remarks provided with the man's mugshot in the West Midlands, England, Criminal Registrar's database on Ancestry.com.

William Edward Collings.

My second great-grandfather.

My grandpa had had the man's nose. Straight with a slightly turned-up tip. Even worse, *I* had the man's nose. I had the nose of a convict. I wasn't about to frame William Collings's mugshot and display it on the fireplace mantel next to my grandparents. Who'd have thought a photo of William Collings *alive* could be more disturbing than one of his wife, Victoria, *dead*?

I took several gulps of wine.

While I'd been searching for William's and Victoria's death records, his criminal record had popped up. He'd been imprisoned for theft. Not a minor theft like stealing a goat for milk or robbing a butcher for meat to feed his starving family. But for stealing jewels and other valuables. Charles *Fitzsimmons's* family jewels, to be precise. One gold watch on a chain, four fur necklets, one emerald bracelet... The list went on and on. I assumed Charles was Williams's father-in-law or other Fitzsimmons relation. Despite having pleaded not guilty, William was sentenced to three years hard labor.

With the assistance of several UK criminal databases on various research sites, I was able to piece together William Collings's background. It turned out that police records had even more useful information than military records. Terrific as long your ancestor was merely serving a fourteen-day sentence for drunkenness. William, a banker, had been born in 1854 in County Cork, Ireland. All the records Michelle had provided noted his birth location as Manchester, England. Errors and inconsistencies were common in historical documents. Yet if any record would be correct, it would be a prison one. With the census or vital records, the person himself could have intentionally provided false information. Why would William Collings have claimed he was born in Manchester if he'd been born in County Cork?

And what had happened to all his money? In the 1911 census, he and his children had lived in a prestigious area of Birmingham. Why had he resorted to robbing his deceased wife's family? An addiction to gambling, drugs, high-end prostitutes... Curious, and desperate to find a justifiable reason behind William's criminal act, I checked for prior convictions. While searching, I came across a 1919 record for a Henry Collings.

My great-grandfather?

I opened the record and discovered it was indeed my Henry Collings charged with assault against Charles Fitzsimmons. He was never sentenced. Not because he was found innocent but because he hadn't been *found,* period. He'd fled Birmingham, and a warrant was issued for his arrest. Was that when Henry and Catherine had escaped to the Isle of Bute with their children and the Fitzsimmons family jewels?

My great-grandfather Henry Collings had been a wanted man.

No wonder my grandparents hadn't told me bedtime stories about Grandpa's family of felons and fugitives. They were no better than Brendan Quigley's sketchy heirs who were thieves and attempted kidnappers and killers! With all these skeletons in my closet, no way would I tarnish Grandpa's memory by going on an episode of the *Rags to Riches Roadshow.* Even worse, what if there were more skeletons? What if Grandpa had followed in his forefather's footsteps and had spent his life hiding out from the law in Ballycaffey?

I had to quit researching while I was ahead!

I should have respected Grandma's apparent wish, which had likely been Grandpa's wish, to not share his family history *before* I'd discovered the prison record!

What about honoring Duncan MacDonald's wish to bury Nancy Drew in my grandparents' graves? I needed to let them both return to Scotland and try to forget this ever happened.

Fat chance that Michelle Thompson and my DNA matches would forget I'd promised them an appearance on the TV show. No way was I following through on that promise.

After polishing off my wine, I snapped a picture of William Collings's mugshot and texted it to Biddy.

My phone rang.

"Ah, that's grand," Biddy said. "A passport photo of your rellie, is it?"

"It's my second great-grandfather William Collings's mugshot."

"Janey," Biddy muttered. "What'd he do?"

"Stole jewels, furs, and other valuables from his wife's family."

Biddy let out a relieved sigh. "Better than him having murdered the entire lot of 'em in their sleep."

"If you're trying to make me feel better, it isn't working. After he was arrested, his son, my great-grandfather, assaulted his grandfather Charles Fitzsimmons, and a warrant was issued for his arrest."

"Both father and son went to prison?"

"Nope. Henry fled, and as far I can tell, he was never captured and imprisoned."

"Well, that's good anyway."

"How's that good?"

"Would rather be having a great-grandfather who'd been an outlaw than a convict. There's a certain mystique surrounding outlaws. Like *Butch Cassidy and the Sundance Kid*. Brilliant movie. Paul Newman was beyond dreamy."

"They won't be making a movie about my family. Not even an episode of the *Rags to Riches Roadshow*."

"No Roadshow filming?" Biddy's voice filled with disappointment. "Already ordered a dress for it."

"I'm not exposing my family's past to Kiernan Moffat and the rest of the television-viewing world. I'm calling the appraiser first thing in the morning."

"Maybe you should sleep on it."

"I doubt that nightmares about my family of felons will be changing my mind." Fuming that Biddy was more disturbed about me canceling the show than my convict ancestors, I hung up.

Moments later Biddy called back.

Despite my better judgment, I answered it.

"Sorry. If it makes ya feel any better, my great-uncle Jimmy McCarthy went to jail a half dozen times. Would have been better for his family if he'd been a fugitive *once* than having been repeatedly convicted for stealing women's knickers and lingerie. And I'm not talking about pocketing women's fancy silk knickers from an upscale boutique. He'd take them straight off a clothesline. My auntie Rose might have been more understanding if he'd been stealing them for her, despite being used, but he was nicking them for himself."

I was in a real funk when one of Biddy's crazy stories couldn't even make me smile.

A text dinged. Finn.

Pub getting ready to close. Ya didn't show for drinks. Everything okay?

I burst into tears.

Seventeen

I LAY IN BED, squinting back sunshine pouring through the skylight. I covered my face with a pillow. *Make the ringing in my head stop.* I was waiting for vertigo to kick in and the room to start spinning. A loud pounding interrupted the ringing. When slapping my hands over my ears muffled the pounding, I realized it wasn't in my head. The noise was coming from outside, below my bedroom window.

I tossed the pillow on the floor and threw back the duvet. I squinted out the window and down at jet-black hair and Gretta's knuckles rapping against the front door. I stepped back from the window before she could look up and see me. What was she doing here at... I glanced at the clock on the nightstand—10:00 a.m. Okay, it wasn't insanely early. Still, it was when I hadn't gotten to sleep until after 4:00 a.m. Every time I'd closed my eyes, William Collings mugshot popped into my head. I hadn't thought anything could be worse than going to bed at night and seeing Duncan MacDonald's haunting gaze staring back at me. I slipped under the duvet and pulled it over my head, planning to stay in bed all day.

My phone chimed on the nightstand. I ignored the text. A few minutes later, it rang. Seriously? I snatched up the phone. Gretta. Her text read: *You won't believe what I found!*

Unless she'd found my ancestors' prison records, I no longer cared. I couldn't imagine Gretta was exactly a computer whiz, so I wasn't too worried about her coming across the photo and blackmailing me. Besides, the old Gretta might have done such a horrible thing, but the new and improved one wouldn't.

Would she?

Regardless, I was done researching Grandpa's family. The identity of Nancy Drew would have to remain a mystery. The future of Duncan MacDonald and the person in the purple pouch was in the hands of Reverend Quinn.

Before turning off my phone, I noticed Finn had replied to my text apologizing for no-showing last night.

No worries. You're grand.

I was far from grand.

I turned off my phone and hid back under the duvet.

My stomach growled. After last night's discovery, I'd been too upset to eat a late dinner and instead had slammed three glasses of wine on an empty stomach. I rolled out of bed and trudged down the stairs to the kitchen. I stuffed a handful of Froot Loops in my mouth while waiting for my tea to brew. Pinky was outside the window, glaring at me eating his treats. I tossed a handful of cereal out the window and onto the lawn. The sheep scarfed up the colorful pieces. The animal's owner probably wouldn't approve of my treats. Kind of like my mom forbidding me to go to Megan Rodgers's house after school when she'd discovered that we'd eat bowls of Lucky Charms and other forbidden sweet cere-

als. I'd go home on a sugar rush too full for supper. The
owner had no right to judge me when he allowed his animal
to wander freely on the roads of Ballycaffey.

I plopped onto the couch with my laptop. Since going to
bed six hours ago, I'd received emails from my Flanagan
cousin Angie and Michelle Thompson. Their DNA was live
on GEDmatch. I tapped a finger against the keyboard.

I'd been desperate to have as many known relations as
possible on the site. Now I was tempted to delete my
account. However, determining my Flanagan and Fitzsimmons matches would enable me to focus on lines likely
linked to my biological father. I might be merely one cluster
report away from identifying him. Yet this entire situation
was a complete *cluster*. Besides, even if I determined that a
group of DNA matches was likely related to one of my
biological father's ancestry lines, it could take months to
figure out that ancestor's identity. I had no known paternal
relatives to link them to. Did I want known paternal relatives? With all my excuses lately, I was seriously starting to
wonder.

Just when I thought I couldn't have been any more overwhelmed, an email arrived from Simon Reese. He'd talked to
his mother, who'd talked to a cousin, who'd confirmed she'd
once been eavesdropping on her parents discussing the
Fitzsimmons family near Cornwall, who'd raised Simon's
grandma Eleanor. The cousin was told to never repeat what
she shouldn't have heard. He promised to forward information on the nice couple who'd raised Grandpa. It was reassuring to know Grandpa had grown up with good parents.
Simon said yep, that was his grandma Eleanor with the
polka-dot dress and long hair in Michelle's photo. And

when and where would we be filming the *Rags to Riches Roadshow* episode? I was on a major guilt trip over letting down Simon and our other relations. But no way was I going to allow Kiernan Moffat to expose our deep dark secrets.

I slapped my laptop closed.

I didn't feel indebted to the appraiser, since he owed me for not tipping off the guards about the role he'd likely played in the Neils' missing manuscript. The man was going to be relentless, trying to convince me to do the episode since he'd helped solve part of my family mystery. Dreading the conversation, I needed to get it over with. After gulping down another cup of tea and polishing off a bowl of Froot Loops, I took the plunge and placed the call.

"Have you spoken with that woman in Down yet?" The appraiser dived right into the conversation, forgoing any greeting or pleasantries.

"I actually drove up and met with Michelle yesterday."

"Ah, brilliant. Were you able to confirm your families are related?"

"Yes, but I—"

"Perfect! After you left the other day, I spoke to the producer, who is on board. I began compiling ideas for the episode straight away. Even though I have plenty of my own, I feel your input would be invaluable. We could collaborate. You would, of course, receive mention in the credits."

"The credits that scroll at the end of the show?" What great exposure for my genealogy business to have such an impressive role on a popular TV show. The minor part I'd played in the episode three months ago had kicked my business into overdrive.

"Of course the ending credits. We should pencil in a date to start reviewing the..."

As he rambled on, reality set in. Exposure for my genealogy business wouldn't offset respecting what must have been Grandpa's wish that his past remain in the past. And many of the show's viewers might think twice about hiring me for fear I'd be exposing the skeletons in *their* closets. Like me, most people didn't foresee a DNA test or traditional research turning their world upside down until it happened.

"I'm sorry, but there's not going to be an episode."

"Everything is negotiable. I'd be happy to share the credit as executive cowriter rather than—"

"It's not that."

"Then what is it? We haven't even discussed the particulars."

"I've decided I'm not comfortable airing a show about my grandfather's family history." *Airing* his dirty laundry was more like it. "He was a very private man. He had a difficult childhood and preferred to keep the past in the past. I need to respect his wishes."

"That's absolute rubbish. You were quite interested the other day. Went to visit that woman within hours of me forwarding her information..." He lowered his voice. "Did you discover something you don't wish to share?"

"No," I blurted out, a bit overly defensive. "I just prefer to keep my ancestry private."

"I doubt Miss...whatever her name is in Down will agree. She has dreamed of being on the show for years. I'm sure she'll still wish to pursue the project with or without your assistance."

My grip tightened around my phone. "Even if it means going against *my* wishes when I'm the only reason you even came up with the idea for the episode?"

"I have the right to move forward with the project. I have the approval of the producer and—"

"Well, you don't have *my* approval. And it wouldn't be in *your* best interest to move forward without it. Or I might move forward with pursuing matters about *you* that you most definitely wouldn't approve of."

Silence filled the line except for nervous gum chewing on the other end.

"I have no idea what you're referring to," he said.

Like the scam he'd most certainly been operating with Valerie Burke prior to her being imprisoned. His clandestine meeting at a Dublin hotel offering Professor Stewart a deal on a stolen manuscript. Giving Aidan Neil the name of a forger in exchange for a percentage of the manuscript's sale. The appraiser had been flying just far enough under the radar to not have been caught.

Since all I had against the man was speculation and theories, I said, "Oh, I think you know what I'm referring to." I disconnected the call with a shaky finger, heart racing over having just threatened one of the dodgiest men I'd ever known!

If Michelle Thompson was resuming her research, what was the chance she wouldn't discover our family's sketchy past? If she subscribed to Ancestry.com, she'd likely come across the UK prison records, which had just recently been added to the site's catalogue. Unlike me, would she be fine sharing our scandalous past with the world? After all, she only had one skeleton, William Collings, whereas I had two, including one a generation closer, my great-grandfather, Henry. Like Biddy, would Michelle believe there was a certain mystique about my outlaw ancestor having to hide out on the Isle of Bute?

Hiding out on the remote island sounded pretty good right about now.

A torrential downpour had just ended when I parked in front of the cemetery's gate. I arrived at my grandparents' graves to find the purple pansies I'd planted drowning in a puddle of mud. Closing my eyes, I inhaled a deep breath, trying to shake it off.

I opened my eyes, peering at my grandparents' tombstone. "Duncan MacDonald, who passed away here, and most likely his wife's remains in the purple pouch, are going to be buried in Scotland." I peered through tear-filled eyes at Grandpa's side of the tombstone, Henry Liam Fitzsimmons. "I'm sorry I didn't honor what was likely your wish that the past remains in the past. But it will from here on out."

Grass rustled behind me. Startled, I turned to find Edmond. I burst into tears.

Edmond wrapped me in a hug. "Sorry, luv. Didn't mean to be scaring ya to tears. Saw your car in the drive and haven't heard from you. Was a wee bit worried."

I wiped the tears from my cheeks, stepping back from Edmond's comforting embrace. I shook my head. "It's not your fault. It's my great-grandfather's." I told Edmond everything, starting with my visit to Michelle Thompson and ending with my felon and fugitive ancestors. How I regretted having opened Pandora's box.

He nodded. "Right, then, that's what Maggie meant about the *key* to the past."

"Do you think she knew all those horrible things? Or just that the locket had been an heirloom for a family Grandpa hadn't wanted to discuss?"

He shrugged. "Who can say for sure?"

"If she did, it hurts that she didn't tell me any of it. She knew I'd have kept it a secret if she'd asked."

"She was likely honoring your grandfather's wish, which would have superseded her desire to always be forthcoming about family history. So this Michelle had a fair amount of background on the family, did she?"

I nodded. "Grandpa's parents, Henry and Catherine, married in Birmingham. Yet at the time, he worked for the post office in London. Well, actually it was a bank... I'm not sure what it was. A Post Office Savings Bank?"

Edmond quirked a curious brow. "At Blythe House by chance?"

I nodded faintly. "Yeah, that was it. How did you know that?"

"I've read most every biography on Michael Collins. He also worked at the Post Office Savings Bank at Blythe House in Kensington."

"As in Michael Collins, who led Ireland to independence?"

He nodded. "At the age of sixteen, he moved to London to live with a sister. He belonged to the clandestine Irish Republican Brotherhood there and became involved with Ireland's cause. Your ancestor's name Collings is an awfully close spelling to Collins. A bit more anglicized, perhaps. It may be purely a coincidence...or it may not."

"Are you saying you think my *Collings* were related to Michael *Collins*?"

"Your William may have been an English relation of Michael Collins and an Irish sympathizer. Or he'd been an Irishman living in England at that time when tensions were at an all-time high. Would certainly have been cause for a name change, even a slight one."

"Where was Michael Collins born?"

"Woodfield, County Cork."

My heart raced. "William's prison record states he was born in Cork, when every other document claims he was born in Manchester."

The corners of Edmond's mouth curled into an intrigued smile. "Interesting indeed."

"One of my DNA test sites lists the top ten locations in Ireland where my ancestors likely lived. Cork was number four. Maybe William Collins changed his name to a more English surname, adding a *g* to help hide his Irish identity from his wife Victoria's snooty parents."

"Maybe also from *her*. If he stole her family's jewels to fund Ireland's fight for independence, would that justify his criminal act?"

"No." I shrugged.

Edmond was right. I shouldn't be so quick to judge my ancestors when I didn't fully know the circumstances. I'd read plenty of divorce transcripts and wills to understand that people had reasons and motivations for their decisions, even though a hundred years later they seemed like bad ones.

"Those were difficult times," Edmond said. "It's hard to

judge a desperate person's actions. The Irish War of Independence was a guerrilla war fought against the British starting in 1919 and lasting over two years. Then in 1922 the Irish Civil War began. When Michael Collins signed an Anglo-Irish treaty accepting less than complete independence for all of Ireland, he feared he was probably signing his death warrant. Sadly, he was right."

A chill raced through me at the thought of my great-grandfather also possibly having been killed while fighting for Ireland's independence. Hopefully, he hadn't been tracked down by the British police and murdered or imprisoned for life.

"My grandpa's dad likely fled England in 1919."

"Might have been easier, and safer, for someone coming from England to go through the back door via Glasgow to Belfast rather than directly from England to Dublin. Perhaps Henry thought it safer to have his family hide out on the Isle of Bute when he was off fighting for the cause in Ireland."

"Maybe my grandpa just happened to have been born on the island when the family was en route to Ireland in 1922. Yet why had Simon's grandma and possibly my grandpa been raised in Cornwall by Fitzsimmons relations?"

"Sadly, your great-grandfather might not have survived the war. Would have been difficult at that time for a widowed woman to raise the children on her own."

"What about the stolen jewels? You'd think he'd have kept a few aside for his wife to sell if he didn't return from war."

"How do you know they weren't recovered earlier by the British police and returned to Charles Fitzsimmons?"

I shrugged. "I don't."

"Henry had both the British military and police after him at that point. Maybe Catherine feared the only way to keep her children safe was to have them live with relations. Will take a look at my history books and ones on Michael Collins. See if I come across a Henry Collings having played a role in the war."

I peered over at the pansies wilted into the mud puddle. Planting Grandma's favorite flowers hadn't hidden the hole that Duncan MacDonald had dug, attempting to bury remains that were likely his wife's. Covering up the past didn't make you forget it. You had to learn to accept it. In this case, acceptance would be made easier if I learned I was related to Ireland's greatest hero!

Eighteen

UPON RETURNING HOME, I flew from the car and toward the house, giving Pinky a wave across the lawn. I was sticking the key in the lock when the arrival of a text dinged. I checked my phone. Finn.

Heading back to Wexford. Keep me posted on the dead fella.

I dropped my head against the door. *Sorry about last night.*

I tapped a finger against the phone, debating if I should text an excuse, call and explain...or quit while I was ahead.

Safe travels home. Call if you need to talk.

Neither one of us mentioned dinner or how we couldn't wait to do it again. If there was one thing dinner had taught me, besides never to wear jeans to a restaurant with iron scroll chairs, it was that for me to have a successful relationship, the guy would have to meet four important criteria.

Number one. Someone I wanted to spend time with as much as I did Biddy.

Number two. Someone who was as passionate about genealogy as I was.

Number three. Someone who lived within an hour's drive from me.

Number four. Someone who didn't like lamb, which might be difficult to find in Ireland. So that one couldn't be a deal breaker.

Right now Finn didn't meet even one requirement.

Helping Finn work through his PTSD was impossible when we rarely saw each other. Not to mention, I wasn't equipped to help him. My mentioning Gretta had triggered his PTSD. What if instead of fixing him, I broke him even more?

I made a strong cup of tea and sank onto the couch with my laptop. I took a deep breath, mentally preparing myself for what I might find. Precisely what I should have done last night before embarking on research that led to finding my ancestors' prison records. I began researching Ireland's civil records index for a Henry Collings who died during the Irish Civil War period.

An entry came up for a Henry Collins who died in Dublin in 1922 at age thirty-seven. That would have been the age of my great-grandfather. It gave the time period of death as January to March. He might have died before my grandpa was born later that year. A copy of the original record was available via email or in person at the registrar's office in Dublin. I'd obtain it later to confirm it was my great-grandfather.

Hopefully he'd died for Ireland's cause rather than the British police having caught up with him. With all the unrest in Ireland at that time, I couldn't imagine the police hunting somebody down for assault. Not like it'd been murder. They'd had bigger concerns than some man having punched out another. Unless Henry had fled with the Fitzsimmons jewels because his father had been imprisoned. I needed to learn where he was buried to ensure he had a proper headstone memorializing his life and death.

Who'd have paid for a headstone? I couldn't imagine that his body had been sent back to the Isle of Bute or that people even knew where to send his body during all the unrest and chaos. It could have been weeks before Catherine had learned of her husband's death.

If the death certificate was my Henry, and Edmond was right that his wife Catherine Drummond couldn't have afforded to raise their children on her own, she'd likely have remarried. If she hadn't remarried soon after her husband's death, maybe she'd had no choice but to send my grandpa and his sister Eleanor to live with Fitzsimmons relatives in southern England. Relations she must have truly trusted after her father-in-law, William, had stolen the Fitzsimmons family jewels.

My heart ached for Catherine, likely having been widowed and left with no means to care for her small children. I couldn't imagine a mother having to send a newborn to live with relatives. Maybe she'd also feared for her children's safety if Henry had played a known role in the war. Besides the fact that he was a wanted man in England. She'd also likely lived in fear that old man Fitzsimmons would hunt them down and seek revenge by taking her children, his grandchildren, from her. Poor Catherine certainly had a lot of stress.

What if she'd remarried and her new husband hadn't

wanted to take on the responsibility of her children? Would Catherine have confided in him about Henry's involvement in the war or taken the secret to her grave? Maybe Grandpa hadn't known about his family's scandalous past but struggled to forget his childhood trauma of never having known his real parents. Based on how Grandma described him, he'd have been the stoic type and kept it bottled up inside rather than seeking therapy for PTSD.

If ever I needed to use a lifeline to phone a dead ancestor, this was it.

I searched Scotland's civil records and found a marriage for a Catherine Collings and Bernard Douglas in February 1923, on the Isle of Bute. Bernard Douglas? That was the father's name noted on Winifred's marriage certificate to Duncan MacDonald. If Catherine had remarried in 1923, that had to be her husband Henry who'd died the previous year when she was pregnant with Grandpa. Winifred had been two or three years old when her mother had married Bernard, so the man had been her stepfather, not her biological one. She must have known her real father's identity and her brother, Liam, my grandfather, if Duncan had been determined to bury the two of them together.

Nancy Drew was Grandpa's sister, my great-aunt Winifred.

A tear slipped down my cheek. Having confirmed her identity, how could I not bury her remains, along with Duncan's, in our family plot? After all these years it had been important enough for Duncan to reunite the two siblings to risk a heart attack while doing so.

I shot an email off to Reverend Quinn offering to take full financial responsibility for Duncan MacDonald's burial in Ireland. Since his congregation was struggling to come up with the funds, he would surely agree to it. It would likely take a chunk of my share of the book advance. My conservatory project was definitely on hold. As were a new mattress for the master bedroom and a shed to protect my new fuel tank.

Upon further research, I found a William Collins born in Cork the year of my William, to a Henry and Eleanor. Even though those were prominent names in my family tree, that didn't confirm this was my William. I checked out online trees for Michael Collins, hoping I could figure out William's connection to one of Michael's relations. There were over three hundred trees just on Ancestry.com. Numerous ones had Michael Collins married with a half dozen kids born between 1912 and 1920. How'd he have that large of a family when he was always off fighting for Ireland's independence? Not to mention, he'd lived in London when half the kids in the trees were supposedly born in Cork. A few trees even had a 1939 English census record attached for some other Michael Collins, when the hero had died seventeen years earlier. The document appeared to be where the Irish hero's supposed children's names had come from.

I called Edmond, who confirmed Michael Collins had never married. He'd been engaged to marry two months after his death. Precisely why you couldn't trust information in an online tree even if a *hundred* trees contained the same details. Ninety-nine trees had been copied from *one* wrong tree. Too bad more people didn't set unverified trees as private, not visible to the public. Or at least tag people in the tree as unverified.

Trusting DNA way more than online family trees, I

decided the best way to connect my family to the Collins in County Cork was clustering matches on GEDmatch. Thankfully, I hadn't deleted my account. Also, if William Collings had indeed come from Cork, that meant my biological father quite possibly wasn't my connection to the county. He could indeed be English, as I'd originally assumed. Based on Simon Reese's DNA, he had no Irish ethnicity. However, a person inherited only 12.5 percent of his DNA from a great-grand-parent. It was a crapshoot what ethnicities were passed on. DNA definitely was not an exact science.

The doorbell echoed through the house.

If I had a clue how to disconnect that thing, I would!

Biddy was at work. Anyone else would have to wait. I was busy proving I was related to the greatest Irish hero of all time! The ringing continued before the person finally gave up. While I was gulping down the rest of my tea, a rap sounded on the living room window. Startled, I spilled tea down the front of my white shirt. Gretta's gray eyes peered under the sliver of window visible below the blind. She was shouting something I couldn't understand. It seemed urgent, and the woman wasn't about to give up, so I answered the door.

Gretta flew past me and into the living room. She thrust a piece of paper at me. "Look at the informant on Lillian Flynn's death certificate in 2011." Gretta waited anxiously while I scanned the record.

"Martha Grady." I shrugged. "I have no clue who that is."

"Her location is more important," she said impatiently.

I squinted at the small print under the woman's name. "Portaferry, County Down."

"Precisely. I looked it up, and the town's population is about twenty-five hundred. Would be awfully coincidental that you were there yesterday visiting that woman and this person isn't somehow related to her."

"Coincidences happen way more than you'd think in genealogy research. Besides, Michelle Thompson's family is related to the Collings side of Grandpa's family, not his maternal Drummond side. Why would one have been an informant on Lillian Drummond Flynn's death record?"

"Precisely the question I'd be asking that Michelle."

I nodded. "I'll shoot her an email."

Bombarded with discoveries, my head was ready to explode. I couldn't even begin to figure out this one on my own. I hoped Kiernan Moffat hadn't already informed Michelle that I no longer planned to film the episode. She might not be nearly as helpful as she had been yesterday.

Gretta smiled anxiously. "What next?"

"I don't really need help at this point."

Her smile faded.

The doorbell rang.

For the love of God!

I answered the door to find Biddy dressed in pink scrubs with unicorns, holding a bag from my former favorite Chinese takeaway place. My stomach didn't hold a grudge and growled at the scent of Kung Pao chicken's spicy peanut sauce.

"You're already off?" I said.

"Got off an hour early." Biddy eyed Gretta standing behind me. "What's *she* doing here?"

"Providing a critical piece of evidence." Gretta gestured to the bag in Biddy's hand. "Rather than takeaway." She breezed out the door, snubbing Biddy as she passed by. "I'll be in touch."

Biddy glared at Gretta walking down the drive, a low growl vibrating at the back of her throat. She headed inside and removed a to-go container from the bag, then dumped a slew of fortune cookies onto the cocktail table. "We'll open them all and choose the best one. Undo the streak of bad luck the missing fortune caused."

"I don't have time to open cookies." I brought Biddy up to speed on the possibility of adding Michael Collins to my family tree.

Biddy's eyes widened. "How bloody brilliant would that be? Being related to the most important figure in Irish history would certainly make up for the convict and outlaw."

I dropped onto the couch and peered at my laptop. "You can only stay if you promise not to talk. I'm trying to confirm my connection to him via DNA matches."

"Promise." Biddy plopped onto the love seat across from me. She tore open a crinkly plastic wrapper and cracked open a fortune cookie. She read the slip of paper. "Ohh, this is a good one."

I gave her the evil eye.

"Sorry. I'll help myself to wine. Fancy a glass?"

"Sure." I handed her the container with Kung Pao chicken. "Stick this in the fridge. I need to concentrate on research, not eating."

I signed into my GEDmatch account. Simon Reese and Angie were my top matches. I ran a report of Simon Reese's and my shared matches. Nearly a hundred came up. From that report I generated a cluster chart. An array of colored squares filled the graph. A large orange square at the top included Simon and several dozen shared matches.

"Those are lovely colors, aren't they now?" Biddy set my wineglass on the table next to my computer. "What do they mean?"

"Once I analyze them, I'll explain. Right now I need to focus."

"Fine. Sorry."

Two profile names in the orange square jumped out at me. Drummond, my great-grandmother Catherine's surname, and *MST*, Michelle Thompson's profile name.

"Hmm..." I muttered.

Biddy perched on the edge of the love seat cushion. "What's *hmm* mean?"

"Neither Simon nor Michelle Thompson should be a blood relation with a Drummond. Only through the marriage of Henry and Catherine. Yet they're showing related. And the informant on Lillian Drummond's death certificate was from Portaferry. Unless this Drummond is merely a coincidence and not related to Catherine. Or is actually a Collings..."

Biddy opened her mouth, and I held up a finger. She collapsed back against the couch and sipped her wine.

I searched a few sites and found a record for a Lillian Collings born 1918 in Birmingham to a Henry and Catherine Collings, mother's maiden name not listed. I checked the UK vital records index, which only listed the mother's maiden name, which was Drummond. No wonder a Lillian *Drummond* hadn't showed up in my previous search for the woman's birth record.

She'd been a Collings, not a Drummond.

"Bingo."

"Bingo, what?" Biddy bounced with anticipation on the cushion. "And don't be hushing me. You can't say something like *bingo* and expect me to keep my gob shut."

"Lillian Drummond Flynn was my grandpa's sister, not a maternal Drummond cousin."

"The woman with the wreath on her grave?"

I nodded. "She must have been sent to live with her mother Catherine Drummond's relations in the UK or Ireland and took their last name. Maybe the children taking on the adopted names had been at their mother's request for their safety. How sad that the siblings were split up at such young ages."

"That's bloody awful." Biddy took a gulp of wine.

I returned to the original report with Simon and my shared matches to identify those who used initials or nicknames for their profile names. Email addresses frequently provided a person's real name or at least a last name. Also, one family member often managed the accounts for several relations and used his address for all of them. That helped determine those who were closely related. An email with the name Emily Cullen was one of the matches. Cullen wasn't a common Irish name. I'd met few Cullens, and the only one I knew personally was Breeda, the owner of Cullen's B & B.

"Holy cats," I muttered. "I have a match with an Emily Cullen. What if she's related to Breeda Cullen? Was that why Breeda wouldn't confirm Duncan MacDonald's wreath? And she's the one who swiped it from the grave, unaware that Gretta had already found it? If she knew where he'd placed the wreath, she knew the Flynns. Even more importantly, she'd *known* Duncan MacDonald."

"And that he was here to dig up your grandparents' graves. I bet Duncan stayed with her because they were somehow related."

My head was spinning.

Biddy polished off her wine and surged from the love seat. "We need to pay our friend Breeda a visit. Can't believe we bought into that whole distraught act of hers. Making us feel guilty when she was the one who should have been feeling guilty for lying to us."

"Before I jump to any further conclusions and confront Breeda, possibly bringing the woman to tears again, I need to connect her to this Emily Cullen."

After fifteen minutes of Googling, I came across an article in the Westmeath paper congratulating Breeda and Andrew Cullen on their fiftieth wedding anniversary. Out-of-town guests at the party had included their *granddaughter* Emily Cullen.

Biddy hovered behind me reading the article. "Guess we'll be paying your rellie Breeda Cullen a visit."

Unless I was related to her deceased husband, Andrew.

It would be great to find a *living* relation for once.

Nineteen

WHEN BIDDY and I arrived at Breeda Cullen's, we made a beeline for the garbage bin alongside the garage. Biddy flipped back the top, releasing the stench of greasy bacon and curry sauce. She gagged while I plugged my nose and yanked out a bag of trash to find a slightly smushed green-and-yellow wreath with Irish writing on a white ribbon.

"What are you doing?" Breeda flew out the back door, wearing a casual green dress and an alarmed expression.

I removed the wreath from the bin.

She came to an abrupt halt, eyeing the cemetery decoration, her sharp gaze softening. Her shoulders sank, and she gestured toward the house. I threw the trash bag back in the bin and closed the top. I placed the wreath next to it, allowing it to air out before returning it to Lillian Flynn's and Richard Flynn's graves.

Breeda ushered us inside without a word. We passed by the sitting room, where two couples were playing cards, and then down the hall to a light-blue kitchen with white cupboards. She closed the door behind us. Two loaves of freshly baked brown bread sat on a cooling rack. The delicious taste of the crunchy crust on Grandma's bread filled my head. The comforting scent reassured me Grandma was there in spirit.

We joined Breeda at a small wooden table in front of a set of French doors with a view of the flower garden.

The woman took a deep breath and eased it out. "I need to tell ya the truth. I'm likely the only one still alive who knows what the truth is. Had been honoring my Andrew's wishes, who had his reasons for not telling Maggie." A tear trailed down her cheek, and she wiped it away. "But it's time your family knew."

Biddy handed her a tissue from a box on the counter.

My heart raced with anticipation and a bit of anxiety. I wasn't sure how much more truth I could handle. I nodded. "I appreciate it."

She fidgeted with the silver Celtic cross around her neck. "When Duncan came to stay, I had no idea he'd planned to steal your locket. I never would have condoned such a thing. He felt it should be buried with his wife's family, seeing as her parents' remains couldn't be scattered on the grave. Especially since Winifred was the last of the five siblings to pass away. He was a bit overzealous digging up your grandmother's grave."

Breeda pushed herself up from the chair. She went over to the counter and flipped the switch on the electric kettle. I wanted to ask if she might have something stronger. If ever there was a time I could have tolerated whiskey, I feared this was it.

"Maggie had approved of all of the siblings' ashes being spread over your grandpa's grave. But certainly not digging it up to bury 'em." She placed three cups with tea bags on the table.

"She knew about his siblings?" I asked.

Breeda nodded, staring out the window.

The kettle whistled, jarring the woman from her thoughts. "Your grandpa Liam was the youngest yet the first of them to pass. The five children had been split up shortly after Liam's birth, so his dying request was that they be reunited as a family after death. They all agreed, including my husband, Andrew." After filling the cups with water, she sat and stirred milk into her steaming beverage.

"So Andrew was my grandpa's sibling along with Eleanor Fitzsimmons, Winifred Douglas MacDonald, and Lillian Drummond Flynn?"

She nodded.

"Do you know if they were related to Michael Collins?"

She nodded once again. "Indeed, but I don't recall exactly how."

No worries. I'd find the connection. A strong sense of Irish patriotism rose inside me. When I was too blurry eyed to research, I was going to binge watch every Michael Collins movie, starting with Liam Neeson's.

"I don't get why my grandma never told me about our connection to Michael Collins and the role my grandpa's father likely played in the Irish rebellion. That was something to be proud of."

"She didn't tell you because she didn't know. Neither did your grandfather. He and his sister Eleanor went to live with their father's cousin down near Cornwall. He was a Fitzsimmons but estranged from the family. The man and Henry had always been close. The couple adopted the children and never told them the truth about their background. On her deathbed, Catherine told Winifred about her brothers and sisters. Winifred located her siblings. She knew their father had died a heroic death in the war but was never told of the family's connection to Michael Collins. Maybe Catherine had planned to tell her more at the time of her death, but it was unexpected, and she went quickly."

"Do you recall what year she died?"

"The early forties."

I slipped the picture Michelle had given me from my purse and placed it on the table. "This is a photo of my grandpa's aunt Elizabeth and her daughter, and I believe my grandpa and his siblings. I'm thinking it was taken in the 1940s. With everyone dressed up, I assumed it was a major event. Possibly it was the first time they had all met."

Breeda smiled, her eyes watering. "It likely was indeed." She identified the five brothers and sisters. "Winifred was two years old when your grandpa was born, and their father died. She was deathly ill at the time, and Catherine needed to nurse her back to health. Catherine had to make the tough decision to have her newborn live with relatives. Was likely why she sent the locket with Liam."

"What a bloody awful decision to have to make," Biddy said, snagging several tissues and setting the box on the table. She handed me one, and we both blew our noses.

"Winifred said Bernard Douglas was a good man. Catherine had already sent the children to live with relatives to keep them safe from Charles Fitzsimmons, or he'd have accepted them as his own." She dabbed a tissue to her eyes. "May I have a copy of this snap?"

"Of course. I'll have one made." I took several sips of tea, allowing Breeda a few moments to continue enjoying the photo. "Had my grandpa known about his grandfather going to prison for stealing his in-laws' jewels and that his father was a wanted man?" I blew on the hot steam rising from the cup, in serious need of a caffeine fix.

Breeda shook her head. "William Collings never stole the jewels."

I lowered the teacup from my mouth. "I found his prison record."

"A few years before Andrew's death, he tracked down a Fitzsimmons relation who knew the truth. Victoria's father, Charles Fitzsimmons, discovered that her husband, William, belonged to the Irish Republican Brotherhood and was indeed Irish, not English, as he'd claimed in order to have the man's blessing to marry his daughter. When Charles learned William was also a relation of Michael Collins and preparing to return to Ireland to fight for the country's independence from Britain, he fabricated the theft story and had him imprisoned."

Biddy snapped back in her chair. "What a nasty man."

Breeda nodded. "Sadly, my husband, Andrew, and Winifred were the only two who were still alive to learn the truth. After speaking with the Fitzsimmons relation, Andrew did extensive research and found the transcripts of the court session when William pleaded innocent and insisted it was a setup by his father-in-law. Andrew also came across an appeal that was denied. Charles Fitzsimmons was a very powerful man."

The woman took a sip of tea followed by a calming breath. "William's son Henry, your great-grandfather, likely confronted

Charles Fitzsimmons about the lies, and the argument escalated. But to answer your question, your grandfather did know about the theft. Sadly, he died not knowing the *truth* about it. While researching William's death, Maggie discovered he'd died in prison. Liam demanded she stop researching and promise to never discuss a word of it again. His childhood had been difficult enough, and he wasn't about to make it even worse."

"How sad that my grandpa died not knowing the truth. If he had allowed my grandma to continue researching, he'd have known what a patriotic and passionate line of men he'd come from. Not a family of felons."

Yet when I'd discovered William's and Henry's prison records, I'd decided to let it go. If it hadn't been for Edmond, I likely would have, and I wouldn't be sitting there right now with Breeda.

"Andrew never told Maggie the truth for fear it would have made her regret not having continued her research despite her husband's request. He didn't want her to have to question her decision and live with that. It seemed like the right thing to do. As did my not telling you because your grandma hadn't even known. But you have the right to know the truth."

I placed a comforting hand on Breeda's. "So had your husband come here to live with Cullen relations?"

The woman smiled. "He and Lillian were raised by Drummond relations in Scotland, yet when he learned the truth about his biological father, he changed his name back to Collins. When he immigrated to Ireland, his papers mistakenly had his name as Cullen rather than Collins. He decided maybe it was a sign to have a fresh start."

A genealogist's worst nightmare. Sadly, similar situations often occurred, and nobody was alive to provide the truth.

I now vowed to always document the truth about our family's history, good or bad.

On the way home from Breeda's, Biddy and I stopped at the Ballycaffey cemetery. I wanted to visit my grandparents' graves and share everything I'd just discovered about Grandpa's family. Heading along the path toward the back, we spotted Gretta still playing caretaker, tidying up decorations blown around by strong winds earlier.

"I should tell her that my family mystery has been solved and thank her for her help."

"She's grand," Biddy said. "Doesn't be needing your recognition." She started walking away.

I headed toward Gretta, and Biddy reluctantly joined me, letting out an annoyed groan. Gretta was kneeling, staring at the bouquet of yellow daffodils in front of the grave, holding one lone flower in her hand. Rather than tending to some random grave, it was her son Richard's, who'd died in the States in 1987 at the age of nineteen. Edmond hadn't known the cause of death when I'd once inquired. As far as he knew, nobody in the area did.

I was about to quietly back away, hoping she hadn't heard us, when Gretta peered up with tear-filled eyes. "He'd have been fifty-three today." She inhaled a deep breath and eased it out, placing a hand gently on the gravestone. "Been gone thirty-four years, but it never gets easier, losing a child."

"I can't even imagine," I said softly, fighting back tears. I'd thought I was cried out after visiting with Breeda.

"And to think I almost took the life of another mother's child with that car accident."

Gretta and Finn both had trauma to work through.

"I didn't want him to go to school in the States, but Thomas told me I needed to let him go." Gretta wiped a tear from her blotchy cheek. "When we took him to the Dublin airport that day and said goodbye, I didn't realize we'd be letting him go...forever."

"Ah, Janey," Biddy muttered, wiping a tear from her cheek.

I swallowed the lump of emotion in my throat.

Gretta peered down at the flower in her hand. "Daffodils were Richard's favorite flower, but not easy to find this time of year, of course. He was twelve when he wanted to plant daffodils from the house to Drumcara. He had to settle for planting them along our road."

My stomach dropped. The daffodils Biddy and I'd hastily yanked by the stems and uprooted at the age of eight. We'd tossed them in my wagon, which had bounced along the pothole-filled road, daffodils flying out. We'd treated the precious flowers no better than a bunch of annoying weeds. No wonder Gretta had gone absolutely mad, hunted us down, and threatened legal action. She should have been the one holding a lifelong grudge, not Biddy and me.

My partner in crime and I burst into tears, sobbing uncontrollably. I went over and hugged Gretta. Biddy joined us for a group hug.

Twenty

TWO WEEKS LATER

I bent down in my black sheath dress and carefully placed the purple velvet pouch in the hole we'd dug on Grandpa's grave. It seemed appropriate to bury Duncan MacDonald and his wife, my great-aunt Winifred Collins in the pouch, in case it held a special meaning for the couple. Maybe he'd proposed to his future wife, surprising her with an engagement ring inside the pouch. Besides, after Biddy's story about the remains scratching Seamus's eye, I wasn't taking the chance of sprinkling remains over the grave to have a gust of wind blow them back on us. Even though no wake was held and Duncan had been cremated, Rosie had insisted on sewing the button on his navy suit jacket and hemming his pants. It was the proper thing to do. Biddy pitched a fit about not having a wake until I told her what I'd paid for the cremation and updated headstone. And if she'd wanted a wake, she could have paid for it.

I smiled at Edmond in his black suit, Rosie next to him in a black dress with a pleated skirt, dabbing tears from her eyes with Edmond's hanky. I nodded at Edmond, his cue to begin. I joined Breeda Cullen and Biddy, who was blowing her nose, mascara running down her cheeks. She was in worse shape than Breeda or me. I'd extended an invite to everyone related.

Michelle Thompson hoped to make it down to visit the family grave next month. It turned out that Martha Grady, the informant on Lillian Flynn's death certificate, was Michelle's aunt, her grandma Delia's daughter. Martha had apparently stayed with a widowed Lillian when she was ill. It'd have been quite a trek for Simon to come over from Cornwell. However, we planned to meet up in the near future. I'd learned that Harriett Neeley, a descendant of Elizabeth and Henry's brother Walter, had sold the family locket to the antique shop in Edinburgh before moving to Australia. Simon had contacted the shop owner, who agreed to explain the delicate situation to the person who'd purchased the locket and ask if he'd be interested in selling it to Simon.

Fingers crossed for Simon.

"We are here today to honor the family of Henry Collins and Catherine Drummond," Edmond said. "The family of a man who sacrificed his life so that his children could live in an independent Ireland..."

I'd asked Edmond to read the eulogy I'd written, because I'd have been a blubbering idiot trying to get through it. However, I planned to read a version of it on the *Rags to Riches Roadshow* episode I'd once again agreed to do. Kiernan Moffat had been so pleased that I'd reconsidered that neither of us brought up my threat to turn him into the authorities. My family story demonstrated that good or bad, you needed to pursue the truth. Especially since what you thought was bad might turn out good. Now knowing the truth, Grandpa could finally rest in peace.

I clutched the locket around my neck. The fact that Grandma had given me the heirloom meant it had been my grandparents' wish for me to pass it on rather than bury it like Duncan MacDonald had planned to do. However, the family deserved a memorial. I'd had a ceramic photo tile of Michelle Thompson's picture with my great-grandpa's sister Elizabeth and all her nieces and nephews mounted onto my grandparents' headstone. The photo had also been included with Duncan MacDonald's, which Reverend Quinn had sent me. Much nicer to have an original than merely a copy. I had the siblings' various surnames along with their real name, Collins, engraved under the photo.

Future genealogists owed me, big time.

After Edmond finished speaking, we each tossed a handful of dirt on top of the purple pouch. A tear rolled down my cheek. Biddy, Breeda, Rosie, and I linked arms. We watched while Edmond finished filling in the grave with a shovel.

"I should have bought Emma Donovan's burial plot." Biddy blew her nose. "Never going to get another deal like that. What if I die tomorrow without a plot?"

"Your parents will make sure you receive a burial," I said.

"What if there are no plots left?"

"Then you can have the plot next to me," I said. "At the rate I'm going, I might never marry." Depressing thought, but at least Biddy and I'd spend eternity laughing.

"And I have an extra plot available." Rosie gave me a wink. She'd informed her daughter-in-law Stella she'd be having to buy her own plot in the Canary Islands. "You will have plenty of options."

That was the test of a true friend. Willing to spend eternity with you.

"I'll be wanting a witty tombstone. Don't want people crying when they visit my grave."

"Here lies Lester Moore, Four Slugs from a 44, No Les, No Moore," I said.

Biddy laughed. "That's bloody brilliant. Just make that up, did ya?"

I shook my head. "Saw it on a headstone in Tombstone, Arizona, when I worked at the Birdcage there one summer." I should have bought a T-shirt with the saying on it.

Biddy smiled. "I have one for your stone. Here lies Mags Murray, who was always great craic, until a goat jumped on her back."

"I certainly better not be taken out by one of Aileen Molloy's goats. I better have my headstone done pronto, along with my obit. I want a granite slab covering my entire grave, big enough to include my family tree."

Breeda nodded. "Ah, that's a grand idea."

"Well then, you best stop researching," Edmond said, grabbing a liquor bottle and five shot glasses from a bag. "Or you will need a much bigger plot."

Biddy frowned. "And there'll be no room for me."

"There's always a spot in my family plot."

"Best not be putting that on your tombstone," Breeda said. "People will be taking ya up on the offer."

Edmond distributed the shot glasses, then filled them

with Scotch from a distillery on the Isle of Bute. The strong woodsy scent filled my head.

We raised our glasses.

"Here's to the Collins family together at last," I said. "Despite all the hardships in their past. May they now be able to rest in peace. And forever savor the taste of peat."

We tossed the liquor from our shot glasses across Grandpa's grave. "Slainte!"

Drops of the golden beverage trailed down over the happy faces on the tombstone's photo. Everyone was all smiles that first time the siblings were together.

And now they were together forever.

When I arrived home, the sun was sinking into a purplish-pink sky in the west. I headed around to the backyard, where Pinky was relaxing under the trellis. I gave him a wave howdy and headed toward the lone ash tree at the back fence bordering a field of cattle. The sheep pushed himself up off the ground and trotted after me.

I opened the fairy door on the tree and removed a pink slip of paper from the cubby behind it. My wish to feel like a local had come true. I'd hosted a large successful gathering at my house. My neighbors proved they would have my back should I ever be accused of murder. And I had overcome my fear of sheep.

I removed a new wish written on a blue slip of paper from my purse and recited the old Irish blessing in Grandma's memory. "May you get all your wishes but one, so you always have something to strive for." I went to tuck the piece of paper into the hiding space, alongside the yellow one with a wish still waiting to be granted.

Pinky snatched the paper from my hand with his teeth.

"Drop that," I demanded.

The sheep took off running across the backyard.

I chased the animal up the narrow road toward McCarthy's pub, recalling a time fifteen years ago when a crazed sheep had been doing the chase. Where was somebody with a camera now? I slowed my pace to a jog. Pinky peered over his shoulder at me and came to a halt. He turned around and released the slip of paper in his mouth, and it floated onto the pavement. I swore he smiled at me as he turned and trotted off toward his field.

I picked up the piece of paper from the road and wiped the sheep's slobber off on my dress. A few teeth marks; otherwise, it was in good shape. I smiled, watching Pinky disappear in the distance.

I definitely felt like a local.

A Mags and Biddy Genealogy Mystery
Book Four

USA Today Bestselling Author
Eliza Watson

Genealogy
Tips & Quips

Genealogy Tips & Quips
Learn About Ancestry Research

Genealogy Research Tips

The following two articles about cemeteries are included in my nonfiction book, *Genealogy Tips & Quips*. In 2018 I began writing a genealogy column for my monthly author newsletter about my personal research experiences. I was writing articles faster than I was publishing newsletters, so I decided to compile them into a book. *Genealogy Tips & Quips* includes fifty articles and two extensive case studies— one about how a paternal DNA test revealed my family's royal lineage and my quest to uncover family secrets.

You can learn more about the book at www.elizawatson.com.

Become a Cemetery Whisperer

Family members and I make an annual spring trip to southwestern Wisconsin to decorate our relatives' graves. I've located many of the graves since 2007, when I began conducting genealogical research. At each cemetery, I share the history of our ancestors who immigrated to America. My mind wanders to their families' graves in Ireland, which my emigrant relations never returned home to memorialize. Thankfully, I've had the opportunity to do so when visiting Ireland.

I've explored dozens of old Irish cemeteries located in the middle of sheep fields, at monastic ruins, and at abandoned churches. I've traversed some rough terrain and once had my foot slip into a sunken grave. I have found the remotely located cemeteries via Google's satellite map, cemetery groundsmen, and area locals. It was thanks to a cousin putting me in touch with an unrelated Coffey gentleman that I discovered our Coffey graves. The family plot with five weathered headstones is located ten miles from where my ancestor was born and baptized. The tombstones enabled me to trace my Coffey family tree back to the early seventeen hundreds—a feat I couldn't have accomplished with Ireland's spotty historical records. The family had apparently originated in that area, then over the years dispersed to surrounding locations.

I haven't been lucky enough to find a family plot for my Dalys from Kilbeggan, County Westmeath. Daly is the twenty-fourth most common surname in Ireland, so researching baptismal certificates has been overwhelming. Peter and Sarah Daly had only two children, making it impossible to utilize the Irish family naming pattern to piece together the tree. However, I assume their firstborn son, Patrick, my second-great-grandfather, was named after his paternal grandfather.

Patrick's brother is buried in Kilbeggan, but I've been unable to locate his parents' grave. They died in 1898 and 1921, so their tombstone is likely not too weathered to read. Like my Coffeys, they might have been buried in an old family plot ten miles from where they'd lived. While in Ireland, I visited a cemetery located just south of Kilbeggan in County Offaly. I found graves for a half dozen Daly families—none of them my Peter and Sarah. I was disappointed, yet the headstones helped me rule out several Peters born to these other families and not mine.

So how will I ever find my Dalys' graves? In the US, a person's burial place is usually noted on the death certificate or in an obituary. Death certificates in Ireland, at least pre-1941, don't list burial locations. I haven't found obituaries there dated before 1940, and few Catholic burial records have survived. I've visited genealogical societies and libraries to peruse cemetery transcriptions compiled by local historians. And I've searched online at Find a Grave, www.findagrave.com, and at BillionGraves, www.billiongraves.com. So, I will continue traipsing through Ireland's cemeteries until I one day locate them.

Walking Among the Dead

WHAT A CEMETERY CAN TELL YOU ABOUT YOUR ANCESTORS' LIVES

I mentioned previously that each spring family members and I make our annual trip to southwestern Wisconsin to decorate our relatives' graves. I've located many of the graves since 2007, when I began conducting genealogical research. I share stories with everyone about our ancestors who immigrated to America, along with stories about more recent relatives. For example, my grandma Flannery was born in the valley behind a cemetery located on what was once part of our family's land. This is why we're related to half the small rural cemetery. And likely why a relative responsible for keeping parishioners cozy warm was forgiven for accidentally burning down the church when stoking the woodstove. The family helped rebuild the church and donated a lovely stained-glass window.

For your first cemetery visit, I recommend bringing along copies of your family trees to share with everyone, aluminum foil for transcribing hard-to-read tombstones, a camera or phone for taking photos, and water and sunscreen, which I never remember.

Say cheese. I likely have more photos of me in Irish cemeteries than all the tourist attractions there combined. Take a photo of the cemetery's entrance so you know where the following gravestone pics were taken. Even most rural cemeteries have a sign at the entrance. If there isn't one, then stand back far enough for a good view of the location. Also take photos of the general area in large cemeteries, including a landmark, such as a unique grave. Most importantly, take headstone shots so you can transcribe the information later.

Network. In a cemetery? I have chatted with numerous locals in cemeteries. In Ireland, a nice man once escorted us from a village cemetery to a remote one located miles away in the middle of a sheep field. Old farm machinery and equipment resembling torture devices filled the deserted homestead's property and had us questioning our decision to follow a stranger to the secluded area. To our relief, it was legitimate. I actually corresponded with the man, who turned out to be a Gavaghan. My ancestor Patrick Coffey's sister had remained in the area and married a Gavaghan. You never know where you might encounter a distant relative.

Meet your ancestors' neighbors. For several years I searched for my ancestor Eliza Butler's sister and finally located her laid to rest two tombstones away from Eliza. Her married name had thrown me off. Check online or visit the local courthouse to determine the maiden names of the women's graves surrounding your ancestors'.

Check for birth locations, not merely dates. Many emigrants included their countries of origin on their tombstones. Of course, only one of mine did, or that would have taken all the fun out of research. However, it was common for the Irish to even note their home county. My Flannery ancestors are buried in an old cemetery with mostly Irish emigrants. I snapped pictures of all the ones from County Mayo, since people tended to move to an area where they knew someone from their homeland.

Discover unknown children. You might find children you were unaware of buried next to their parents. Knowing the year each child was born and his spot within the family tree is critical for ethnicities—such as Irish, English, and Scottish—that adhered to a traditional family naming pattern. Adding one name could alter everyone's relation, especially if you discover a firstborn son or daughter that would have been named after a grandparent.

Find extended family members. Search the entire cemetery for your surname, not merely the surrounding area, especially if it's an uncommon name in a rural area. Growing up, my mother didn't think she was related to other Flannerys in nearby towns. However, my genealogical research confirmed that all the families descended from one family that came to the area in the 1850s. They'd originally settled twenty miles from my mom's hometown, and families slowly dispersed over the years. Once you've documented all shared surnames, use the oldest person's information to check online for a family tree or vital records that might provide a clue to a possible family connection.

Travel back in time. Most of my ancestors lived in rural areas both here and in Ireland. However, I had to venture to Chicago to research the graves for my Watson and Turney ancestors. Most Chicago death notices provided funeral and burial information. They'd announce where the carriage procession or funeral train would depart from for the cemeteries located outside of the city and when. What a depressing train ride that must have been, loaded with grieving passengers. Rosehill Cemetery on the northside of Chicago still has the casket elevator that raised the coffin from the train to the cemetery's ground level. The stables also still exist that once housed the horses that delivered the caskets to the burial sites. I was able to clearly envision my grieving ancestors' experiences.

Location, location, location. Many of my Chicago Watson ancestors merely leased burial sites for a set number of years, so no tombstones were erected, or temporary ones were removed when their leases ran out. When a lease is up, some cemeteries allow it to be renewed, while others do not if space is limited. Remains are either removed from the grave and placed in an ossuary (a container or room in which remains are stored), or the new tenant is placed atop the existing one. I'd never heard of such a thing. I have no children. Who would renew my lease? I better make darn sure I purchase a permanent plot. I'm obsessed with cemeteries, and the thought of being kicked out of one is a bit unsettling.

The Rosehill Cemetery office provided me a map detailing the location of my Turney ancestors' graves. It was a poorer area of the cemetery, and over the years, grave markers had become buried beneath the grass. How sad was that? Yet I guess it wasn't as sad as my poor ancestors being evicted from their resting spots. The map directed me to the graves' locations using landmarks and the approximate number of steps to take in which direction. When I arrived at my final destination, using my fingers, I dug up a layer of soil and grass to reveal a small memorial plaque with my ancestor's name and death date. I cleaned the slabs and left flowers on the graves. I recommend adding a shovel to your list of cemetery supplies. Or maybe a spade. Carrying a shovel through a cemetery might attract a bit of unwanted attention.

Author's Note

Thank you so much for reading *How to Handle an Ancestry Scandal*. If you enjoyed Mags and Biddy's adventures, I would greatly appreciate you taking the time to leave a review. Reviews encourage potential readers to give my stories a try, and I would love to hear your thoughts. My monthly newsletter features genealogy research advice, my latest news, and frequent giveaways. You can subscribe at www.elizawatson.com.

Thanks a mil!

About Eliza Watson

When Eliza isn't traveling for her job as an event planner or tracing her ancestry roots through Ireland and Scotland, she is at home in Wisconsin working on her next novel. She enjoys bouncing ideas off her husband, Mark, and her cats, Frankie and Sammy.

Connect with Eliza Online
www.elizawatson.com
www.facebook.com/ElizaWatsonAuthor
www.instagram.com/elizawatsonauthor

CPSIA information can be obtained
at www.ICGtesting.com
Printed in the USA
BVHW020231281222
655124BV00021B/267